DARK MATTERS
And Other Plays

Dark Matters
Laws of Sympathy
Wallowa: The Vanishing of Maude LeRay

By

Oliver Mayer

With an Introduction by Velina Hasu Houston

NoPassport Press
Dreaming the Americas Series

Dark Matters and other plays

Book Design: Caridad Svich and Patrick Danner

NoPassport Press: Dreaming the Americas Series
First edition 2012 by NoPassport Press
PO Box 1786, South Gate, CA 90280 USA;
NoPassportPress@aol.com
www.nopassport.org
ISBN: 978-1-300-15055-8

NoPassport

NoPassport is a Pan-American theatre alliance & press devoted to live, virtual and print action, advocacy and change toward the fostering of cross-cultural diversity in the arts with an emphasis on the embrace of the hemispheric spirit in US Latina/o and Latin-American theatre-making.

NoPassport Press' Dreaming the Americas Series and Theatre & Performance PlayTexts Series promotes new writing for the stage, texts on theory and practice and theatrical translations.

Series Editors:
Tony Adams, Jorge Huerta, Mead K. Hunter, Randy Gener, Otis Ramsey-Zoe, Stephen Squibb, Caridad Svich (founding editor)

Advisory Board:
Daniel Banks, Amparo Garcia-Crow, Maria M. Delgado, Randy Gener, Elana Greenfield, Christina Marin, Antonio Ocampo Guzman, Sarah Cameron Sunde, Saviana Stanescu, Tamara Underiner, Patricia Ybarra

NoPassport is a sponsored project of Fractured Atlas, a non-profit arts service organization. Contributions in behalf of [Caridad Svich & NoPassport] may be made payable to Fractured Atlas and are tax-deductible to the extent permitted by law. For online donations go directly to https://www.fracturedatlas.org/donate/2623

ACKNOWLEDGEMENTS

For DARK MATTERS:
to Clifford V. Johnson, professor of physics, USC, for his expert consultation
to the Alfred P. Sloan Science & Technology Initiative for its award
to the Rosemary Branch Theatre, London; the Pasadena Playhouse, CA; the Magic Theatre, San Francisco; the Los Angeles Theatre Center.; the Blank Theatre, CA., the Horace Mann Theatre at Columbia University, NYC; the Theater Arts at Caltech Playwriting Series; and The LAByrinth Theatre Company for developing the play.

For LAWS OF SYMPATHY:
to Second Stage Theatre, NYC; the NewPowerPlays at the West Coast Ensemble, and Playwrights Arena, Los Angeles, for developing the play.

For WALLOWA:
to the College of Palm Desert Theatre Festival
to Son of Semele Ensemble, Los Angeles

8

SPECIAL THANKS TO

Howard Stein
Gloria Mayer
Velina Hasu Houston
Luis Alfaro
The USC School of Theatre
Don Boughton
The Son of Semele Ensemble
Jon Lawrence Rivera
Playwrights Arena
Elizabeth Canavan
Stephen Adly Guirgis
LAByrinth Theater Company
Caridad Svich
Patrick Danner
NoPassport Press

y mi mas bella flor
Marlene Forte

"Yo no sé por qué estoy mirando
por qué estoy amando,
por qué estoy viviendo
Yo no sé por qué estoy llorando
por qué estoy cantando,
por qué estoy muriendo"

Silvio Rodriguez, "En mi calle"

About the Author

Oliver Mayer is the author of over 25 plays, including FORTUNE IS A WOMAN, about the life and work of Machiavelli. "The Hurt Business: a Critical Portfolio of the Early Works of Oliver Mayer, Plus," is published by Hyperbole Books. "Oliver Mayer: Collected Plays" is published by NoPassport Press, and his play DIAS Y FLORES is featured in "Envisioning the Americas: Latina/o Theatre & Performance," also published by NoPassport Press.

Oliver wrote the libretto for the opera AMERICA TROPICAL, composed by David Conte, published by E.C. Schirmer and Sons. His literary archive is available through the Stanford University Libraries. An associate professor with tenure at the University of Southern California's School of Theatre, Oliver is the winner of a USC Zumberge Individual Award and a Mellon Mentoring Award for Excellence in Faculty Mentoring of Undergraduates.

Truly Alive: Chosen by the Stage

A Preface by Velina Hasu Houston

Spanish playwright, poet, and director Federico García Lorca defined *duende* as "the mystery, the roots that cling to the mire… a force not a labour, a struggle not a thought… the blush of all that is truly alive…."[1] Noting the view of an old guitar *maestro*, García Lorca stated that *duende* is not a question of skill but something that surges up from the soles of the feet.[2] In an article in the *Los Angeles Times*, Oliver Mayer talks about the realization of *duende* in song and onstage. In song he says it is not the beauty of a voice "but when that voice tears, scorches, robs itself of the security of technique and opens in the unknown" – akin to what his character, Lucha, says about the truth of dark matter in Oliver's play *Dark Matters*. Onstage, Oliver describes *duende* as something that "rises to edgy, inexplicable urges… applauds impossible unions… resides in irrational fears, oversized desires and long-buried secrets."[3]

ENDNOTES FOR VELINA HASU HOUSTON'S PREFACE

[1] "Theory and Play of The *Duende*." García Lorca, Federico.
Translated by A.S. Kline © 2007 All Rights Reserved. Downloaded March 10, 2012 @
http://www.poetryintranslation.com/PITBR/Spanish/LorcaDuende.htm.
[2] Downloaded March 10, 2012 @
http://www.poetryintranslation.com/PITBR/Spanish/LorcaDuend e.htm.

[3] "The redeeming demon." Mayer, Oliver. *Los Angeles Times*,

Over the last twenty years, I have seen ten of Oliver's plays in production, from *Blade to the Heat* to his most recent accomplishment, *Fortune Is A Woman*. Others I have read. In his work, Oliver's voice truly rises up from the soles of his feet with the fresh sensations that García Lorca described in his essay about *duende*.

During a visit to Spain after a night of wandering around with his wife, the gifted actress Marlene Forte, seemingly lost but eventually finding their way, Oliver mused:

> "This is a lot like writing a play… the finding of the way *is* the play – the way it feels and how it tests everyone involved – writers, actors, audience – so that they see in a snapshot, and feel in a heartbeat, who they are at that chosen moment. The finding of the play is the style, the tone, the pace, of the play itself. And the getting there is the story – partly GPS'd to be sure – but essentially made new and human by the

---

August 14, 2005.

beautiful and horrendous mistakes made along the way."[4]

Oliver continues in the finding of the way via emotion, discovery, and the confronting of challenges and tests. He does not take the easy path. The theatre can be grateful for that. We should accept no less.

This collection includes *Laws of Sympathy, Dark Matters,* and *Wallowa: The Vanishing of Maude LeRay,* the first two being plays I have not only read but also seen.

Laws of Sympathy is a powerful exploration of immigrant (of color) acculturation amid the complexities of US racism, cultural apprehensions, religious intolerance, and commerce. Two Muslim Bantu women – Jaspora and her mother Mrs. Abdekadir – who survived slavery, rape, and prostitution in their native Somalia strive to carve out a life for themselves in Atlanta with the help of two refugee resettlement aides from the North, Mohammed, an acculturated Sri Lankan American, and Betty. Both aides are disillusioned about life in the US, particularly with regard to people of African descent or Muslims. In addition, Mohammed is infatuated with the strikingly beautiful Jaspora and Betty is crushing on Gerald, a former star

---

[4] "Stages." Mayer, Oliver. January 8, 2011

international athlete disgraced by a drug scandal, who desires Jaspora for both love and profit. He sees her as an Iman for the new age, the face for a new African clothing line that he hopes will rebuild his image and bank account. With sharp-edged tenderness and merciless truth, Oliver explores the two Somali women's attempts at acculturation and the realities of their harsh past that come to light. Oliver handily captures the curious and awkwardly courageous movement of Jaspora into the vagaries of American life and young love American-style as she shifts from her traditional Somali robes to revealing outfits and begins to engage with Gerald. The secondary characters lend a great deal to the texture of the story, too. There is something quite compassionate and beautiful about Betty who wants to believe in the former celebrity myth of Gerald as if she, too, like the immigrants, is seeking an American Dream that does not exist in a real sense, that is always stimulated and simulated to appear glossy for the masses. When Betty cries about Gerald's lost honor (and indeed her lost dream) he says, "Guess I must have struck a national nerve somehow." That nerve is the disintegration of dreams in the necessary engagement with reality that survival demands.

Wallowa was written in collaboration with Los Angeles-based Son of Semele theatre company. It investigates the intricacies of loss and its impact on the transformation of identity when a seventy-six-year-old woman, Maude, is lost in forested mountains. In the Wallowa community, her husband Howard, suspected of foul play, keeps her alive in his memory, while the Sheriff hunts for her briefly, too soon believing her to be dead. "She will be found," he states at the end of Act I, "But we just have to face reality. She's gone to God now." It is an official view that represents the dimension of society that gives up too easily, that Howard and other townspeople are not willing to accept. Howard relies on memory to uphold an intimacy that he hopes will not allow others to dismiss or forget his wife. He states, "Just because 'she's of a certain age' people are supposed to disappear? You're giving up because at 70 she's close to death anyway? My wife's got more life in her than any of you... I look at Maude, and I see her just the way she was when we first met. If you saw her the way I do, you wouldn't be giving up on her." Howard is not the only one wrestling with memories. His daughters are as well, but in different ways that demand they look inside of themselves. Fearing the worst, they reflect upon Maude the woman beyond Maude the mother who reared them. Carrie says of her mother, "I feel like I don't know her! I never asked questions. And now I'll never know the answers." Her sister Marty responds with, "Maybe she didn't want you to know." Perhaps for the first time they must think about their mother as a human being with a history, a life as secret to them as the tangled crevices of the mountains. Townspeople push instinctively, inspired by the spirit of the Nez Perce who once inhabited Wallowa, to continue to search for Maude. Magic in the forest and in the human heart contribute to the search for the missing woman – and the search for self in a world where the grandeur of humanity has been reduced to minutiae and the understanding of who we are, who we love, and what life truly is must be defined by one's wits. Talk about soles of the feet.

Dark Matters strikes me as an interesting exploration of the dark side of human behavior in two critical arenas – that of science and that of love. The key figures are Pedro, a physicist who is behind in publishing his theories regarding supersymmetry or SUSY; Goodnight, a physicist who concurrently (and in fact one step ahead of Pedro) developed a SUSY theory and devised a commercial application for it; and Lucha, a backup singer for famous singers who lives in their shadows, which is sometimes to her liking and sometimes not. Shadows, after all, leave one in the dark. Pedro and Lucha are lovers who believe themselves to be bound for marriage. He equates their meeting with particle physics, as if their meeting and becoming attached (and the alacrity of it) are parts of the gradual creation of the Theory of Everything. He calls her the "superpartner of equal mass" and intimates that they are "two particles on a collision course" and that she is "the most mysterious part of my galaxy." The trajectory of their love challenged by Pedro's lust for SUSY, especially in the face of Goodnight's discoveries, put us face to face with the dark matters of human relationships. Issues such as trust, loss, and belonging in a steadily and dynamically evolving world confront the characters and ultimately us as audience. With regards to science, competition and identity are at the core of Pedro and Goodnight's journeys. Goodnight is poised for immediate change and success with what Pedro calls an "infuriating ease" while Pedro wonders how all of their particularity of scientific ideology truly fits into the universe of human existence. He states, "Faith is the sticky part. The world watching, the pressure rising as another day goes by without any of us being able to prove that TOE[5] is anything other than a match-stick palace of pretty equations – that any of this really finally *matters*." Pedro views Goodnight as going "Hollywood," and feels that Goodnight's use of SUSY is a misappropriation and cheapening of the science. Their competition brings them to dark matters in their association as scientists, but also in their association as men. They tussle in science and internally, but it is Lucha, the artist, who sees the true dark matter of humanity. She states: "Maybe that's all that dark matter really is.... What you're afraid of. What you want.... When the voice cracks, tears – when technique falls away and you're left unmasked alone, with nothing to fall back on that you can see or know." The play questions who is really singing and what could the song mean, throwing us into a gnarly mess of power, loss, and boundaries of identity that

---

[5] Theory of Everything.

fluctuate betwixt and between those questions and their myriad answers.

There are other significant dimensions of Oliver's playwriting career that deserve admiration and acknowledgment.

One is his dedication to a life in the theatre and a life of the mind. As he notes, "Part of a life in the theater is that you never quite disconnect from it, no matter how far away you may venture from your chosen stage – or, to be more accurate, the stage which chooses you."[6] The stage chose Oliver and he answers back by seeking his way in his own inimitable and courageous style. He decries reductive voices in theatre that see the world through a self-made prison[7] and seeks the panoramic view that can be obtained only by opening oneself to beauty and danger, torpedoes be damned – hence the "hurt business" of which he speaks and that is the title of his first collection.

Another important dimension is Oliver's fearlessness in creating worlds populated by people of color. Unlike many American playwrights, he does not live or view the world narrowly as if all the important

[6] "Stages." Mayer, Oliver. January 8, 2011

[7] "Playwright Oliver Mayer: A Profile." Salcedo, Raymond. Downloaded March 10, 2012 @ http://sdsupress.sdsu.edu/EyeStuff/602-2000/mayer.html.

events and stories can only be of European or European American origin or as if the world is monochrome. As he notes, "one thing you can always count on with a play of mine and that is there's going to be a lot of people of color in it."[8] Oliver sees the colorful reality of human existence and refuses to ignore it despite any ethno-cultural myopia that may be reflected in the perspectives of his peers. He is not afraid of history, of his own rich biracial and bicultural heritages, or of the ethnically diverse world outside of our doors. He, in fact, opened the door a long time ago.

Lastly, I recognize a strikingly notable dimension to Oliver's life in the theatre – his commitment to mentoring emerging playwrights. We have been colleagues in this effort since 2003 when he joined me at the University of Southern California School of Theatre in the graduate dramatic writing program that I created in 1990. The love and vigor he brings to nurturing developing writers is selfless and generous. Besides teaching undergraduate and graduate writing students, he also serves as Resident Faculty Master at Parkside International Residential College, overseeing the university experiences of countless students from around the world.

---

[8] "Playwright Oliver Mayer: A Profile." Salcedo, Raymond. Downloaded March 10, 2012 @ http://sdsupress.sdsu.edu/EyeStuff/602-2000/mayer.html.

The theatre should not be without the poetic escapes from this world that García Lorca described, escapes in which authentic emotion and lyricism marry with style and story to reflect upon life and living so that we can continue to discover. Oliver Mayer is in search of the pulse in humanity's marrow. As he says in the essay "The Redeeming Demon" (*Los Angeles Times*, August 14, 2005), he is searching for "extremity, for boiling points, in each character as well as in the greater story."

May the search continue with robustness, inquisitiveness, and mettle, and the subsequent discoveries feed and cultivate the theatre. I have no doubt because Oliver has staying power and there is *duende* in his organic GPS.

DARK MATTERS

By

Oliver Mayer

CAST:

Pedro Enamorado

Aaron Goodnight

Lucha

TIME:

The recent past.

PLACE: A region known both for its universities and its high tech sector.

This play was the winner of the Magic Theatre/Alfred P. Sloan Science & Technology Initiative Award, 2006.

Special thanks to Clifford V. Johnson, USC professor of physics and astronomy, for his consultation on particle physics.

Dark Matters was most recently presented in July 2012 at the LAByrinth Theater Intensive at Connecticut College, directed by Elizabeth Canavan, with the following cast:

Lucha Marlene Forte
Enamorado Max Casella
Goodnight Kevin Geer
Musician Carlo Alban

Although described in the text as the cello, feel free to use another instrument. In previous workshops, we have used a violin and a guitar. In the best of all possible worlds, the cello is preferable, because it resembles the *timbre* of the human voice.

SCENE 1

SFX: Live Cello.

SFX: A scissors snipping.

LUCHA: Don't move.
ENAMORADO: They've gone wild! I wish they'd grow that long on my scalp! I'm starting to look like George Bernard Shaw!
LUCHA: Shaw was hot, in a mad professor kinda way. Like you. My Mad Professor. My noble man.

SFX: Scissors snips.

LUCHA: I've been around a lot of pretty people. A lot of rich people. But – until you-- not so many smart people. I mean really smart people. Don't laugh. It's all about discovery.

ENAMORADO: And that's sexy?

LUCHA: By definition.

ENAMORADO: I'll tell you what's sexy.

LUCHA: What's sexy is the way you dream. My String Theorist! My poet!

ENAMORADO: Poet? Not quite.

LUCHA: (kisses him) Oh yeah?

ENAMORADO: Well, when you put it like that. Poet! Just that my poems happen to be in the realm of particle physics. And my dreams happen to be all about SUSY.

LUCHA:(stops kissing) Suzie?

ENAMORADO: Don't be jealous.

LUCHA: Who the hell is Suzie?

ENAMORADO: Hey, hey. SUSY. It's an acronym.

LUCHA: Acronym my ass --

ENAMORADO: For Supersymmetry! Put the scissors down.

LUCHA: That's not sexy.

ENAMORADO: No, it's not. But the idea is beautiful. SUSY is a component of String Theory. It's part of a larger quest, maybe the largest quest there is. To unify everything we know. We call that TOE -- Theory of Everything.

LUCHA: That one's sexier.

ENAMORADO: C'mon, you must have heard me talk about SUSY before.

LUCHA: I didn't listen till now. (slight pause)
You write her poems?
ENAMORADO: Highly mathematical poems.
LUCHA: Tell me one.
ENAMORADO: Well,..they're hypothetical.
LUCHA: Things exist or they don't, Pedro.
ENAMORADO: They involve extra dimensions.
LUCHA: More than three?
ENAMORADO: Good God, yes. Twenty-six, actually.
LUCHA: How long is this gonna take? I gotta be
across town, --
ENAMORADO: I gotta go too, -- (BEAT) Recording
sesh?
LUCHA: (murmurs yes, then) Teaching?
ENAMORADO: Institute. I have to go introduce a
guest speaker.
LUCHA: Another friend of Suzie's?
ENAMORADO: Aaron Goodnight. He wanted my
job, we interviewed the same day. Haven't seen him
since.
LUCHA: Sounds awkward.
ENAMORADO: We're professionals. We'll share a
clammy handshake and get down to the science and
equations. (laughs) Poor guy hadn't shaved in
months. Same baggy pants and wrinkled corduroy
jacket. No wonder I got the job.
LUCHA: Your corduroy was pretty lived-in the day
we met.
ENAMORADO: (kisses her) Being with you has had a
very nontrivial effect upon me.

LUCHA: I never thought myself trivial.

ENAMORADO: What I mean is,...well, you're just not a simple task at all. I guess feeling isn't. There's a decided absence of visible evidence of the way I feel. I just feel. And that's new for me. I mean we're magnetized. We meet by accident at the DMV, two particles on a collision course, and KAPOW! Haven't slept apart since. Three months! You've become not only the center but the most mysterious part of my galaxy.

LUCHA: I love you too. (BEAT) Pedro? Tell me.

ENAMORADO: Tell you what?

LUCHA: Tell me about Suzie.

SFX: CELLO MUSIC returns as —

ENAMORADO: Don't you have to be across town? Sure it won't be a turn-off?

LUCHA: Quite the opposite.

ENAMORADO: O-kay.... Every particle has a superpartner of equal mass.

LUCHA: Superpartner?

ENAMORADO: Like a girlfriend. Fermions make up matter, and bosons create the forces acting on matter. SUSY says that every boson has a fermion, and every fermion has a boson.

LUCHA: Like us!

ENAMORADO: Except you're not my girlfriend! We're *affianced*! You're my *fiancee*.

LUCHA: I'm your fermion!

ENAMORADO: I'm your boson. We're superpartners. And superpartners have equal mass.

LUCHA: Superpartners have superpowers. Like *"The Incredibles!"*

ENAMORADO: You might say. But there's a sticky field that particles go through. A glue, a molasses sea. The stickiness is mass. Every particle has a superpartner of equal mass. Except that Supersymmetry is broken somehow. Equal mass got messed up when the universe was younger. This is the mess we see now.

LUCHA: I thought this mess was our life.

ENAMORADO: I can handle a little mess.

LUCHA: It's a good poem.

ENAMORADO: How do you know?

LUCHA: Because I don't know what it means. Except, somehow, I do. (BEAT) Be brilliant.

ENAMORADO: Beautiful.

LUCHA: Don't move.

SFX: Scissors snip.

LUCHA: There's a zillion of them.

SCENE 2

SFX: CELLO music stops mid-phrase.

Split scene. Lucha enters a sound-proofed booth. Headphones and a high-level microphone. We hear MUSIC, but in a muted way, the way excess sound bleeds out from headphones. She SINGS BACK-UP to a Leonard Cohen song. On playback:

MALE SINGER:
NOW I'VE HEARD THERE WAS A SECRET CHORD
THAT DAVID PLAYED,
AND IT PLEASED THE LORD
BUT YOU DON'T REALLY CARE FOR MUSIC,
DO YA?
IT GOES LIKE THIS
THE FOURTH, THE FIFTH
THE MINOR FALL, THE MAJOR LIFT
THE BAFFLED KING COMPOSING HALLELUJAH

Lucha sings LIVE:

LUCHA:
HALLELUJAH
HALLELUJAH
HALLELUJAH
HALLELUJAH

SFX: Sounds of a men's urinal. As Enamorado pees at a urinal, A HANDSOME MAN relieves himself at the next urinal. As they pee, --

HANDSOME MAN: Hi.
ENAMORADO: I wasn't -- I didn't mean -- I was in my head -- I mean I hate that when somebody sneaks a peek at me, it's a violation, I mean it's hard enough
—

32

HANDSOME MAN: Professor Enamorado?

ENAMORADO: Yes. I'm sorry, I don't know you. Are you here for tonight's guest speaker?

HANDSOME MAN: I am the guest speaker.

ENAMORADO: Professor Goodnight? Sorry I didn't recognize you! What a pleasure!

GOODNIGHT: The pleasure's mine.

ENAMORADO: You don't mind if I call you Aaron?

GOODNIGHT: Please do, Pedro.

ENAMORADO: You look -- great!

GOODNIGHT: New suit.

SFX: Goodnight zips up.

GOODNIGHT: I've been reading about your new work.

ENAMORADO: Have you? I'm ashamed to say I'm not up on your recent stuff. The last three months have been a real departure for me.

SFX: Enamorado zips up.

GOODNIGHT: Me too.

ENAMORADO: Something came up and took my complete attention. I'm behind on all my reading and most of my research, --

GOODNIGHT: You had a Eureka moment.

ENAMORADO: Did I?

GOODNIGHT: How often does Newton's proverbial apple fall on someone's head these days? And when it falls, who's to say where it lands? And on whose head? Why not here?

SFX: Flushes.

ENAMORADO: Here?

SFX: Flushes.

GOODNIGHT: I saw it.
ENAMORADO: What?
GOODNIGHT: Newton's tree. This summer in Cambridge. It was a very pretty tree, a very youthful 400 year old apple tree. But no apples.
ENAMORADO: Probably waiting for Newton.
GOODNIGHT: And yet, no one was sitting under it, asking for the apple to fall. So I sat beneath the tree. Because it's time to finally find out if our beautiful ideas have been just pissing in the wind.
ENAMORADO: Or not.
GOODNIGHT: Or not!
ENAMORADO: Faith is the sticky part. The world watching, the pressure rising as another day goes by without any of us being able to prove that TOE is anything other than a match-stick palace of pretty equations -- that any of this really finally *matters*.

SFX: Enamorado washes hands.

ENAMORADO: I'm guessing this isn't the subject of your talk today?

GOODNIGHT: I have some good ideas about SUSY breaking and extra dimensions.

ENAMORADO: Talk about sticky stuff.

GOODNIGHT: A molasses sea. (ENAMORADO reacts) I also have a new idea or two about dark matter.

ENAMORADO: I'm working on something similar myself.

GOODNIGHT: I know. (BEAT) See you out there.

Goodnight walks out.

ENAMORADO: Hey, aren't you going to wash your - -?

Enamorado dries his hands.

As he does, MUTED MUSIC as LUCHA sings a perfect take.

LUCHA:
HALLELUJAH
HALLELUJAH
HALLELUJAH
HALLELUJAH
> (breathes as she concludes;
> to herself)
Beautiful.

SFX: Sound of her lighting up a one-hitter and sucking it up.

SCENE 3

ENAMORADO: He is so fucking handsome! And that's not a word you usually use in conjunction with a string theorist!

LUCHA: You're handsome.

ENAMORADO: I mean handsome.

LUCHA: What about the corduroy?

ENAMORADO: Linen. Crisp. And this godlike way of talking about the work we do. This infuriating ease! I mean, face it, it's not digging ditches, but physics is work! I'm preparing my class lectures, plus all the documentation for the Institute. I'm working with three very keen graduate students and when I have a free moment I'm writing on the blog. Plus, my big invited paper for that journal is overdue -- way overdue. I'm chipping away at one of the Himalayas! And with every chip this Himalaya might be about to fall on my head!

LUCHA: Just don't let it fall on the bed.

ENAMORADO: So then this physics heartthrob follows up my peremptory introduction, and wows the entire Institute with at least two new ideas -- at least one of which is in direct contradiction with my latest paper –

LUCHA: The one that's overdue?

ENAMORADO: Maybe I won't finish it now.

LUCHA: Don't talk like that.

ENAMORADO: For a second, I thought he was about to scoop my idea. Then he veered off on some flashy tangent. He's obviously brilliant at everything, the cad. But he must have an Achilles Heel somewhere.

LUCHA: If he's human.

ENAMORADO: And I'm sitting there, with the Dean just behind me, and my best students laughing at his every joke and checking out his ass when he turns around to write on the board -- of course he's got a nice one! -- and I can't stop thinking, *this fucker took a piss and didn't wash his hands*! I smelled my own soapy fingers and I felt victory! Some God! Justice preserved. But there is no justice. I'm meat! Goodnight makes me look like a schlub!

LUCHA: Don't be paranoid!

ENAMORADO: Just because you're paranoid, doesn't mean they're not out to get you! I learned that in the Bronx tenements. Don't ever relax. Nothing good lasts.

LUCHA: Nothing?

ENAMORADO: I can't figure out what he's doing here.

LUCHA: Did you ask him?

ENAMORADO: You don't just go ask somebody! This is chess -- not checkers! (BEAT) Boy am I glad he didn't steal my idea about MACHOs and WIMPs.

LUCHA: Come again?

ENAMORADO: WIMPs -- weakly interacting massive particles, and MACHOs – Massive Compact Halo Objects. Big question which rules the universe. And how.

LUCHA: (laughs) Wimps and Machos?

ENAMORADO: In relation to dark matter haloes.

LUCHA: Oh, these are friends of Suzie's.

ENAMORADO: Acronyms, yeah. Physics people think MACHOS are dead, but I found a way to bring them back. (off her laughter) It's a very good idea.

LUCHA: What about WIMPS?

ENAMORADO: WIMPs interact via the gravitational and weak forces, --

LUCHA: Gravity is a wimp?

ENAMORADO: Gravity is weak. In relation to all the other quantum mechanical forces.

LUCHA: It's not macho like you.

ENAMORADO: I'm not macho. (she giggles) How was your night?

LUCHA: Better than yours. I laid down a perfect take. It only lasted a moment, but it felt....beautiful. At my age, you learn to treasure those moments. My voice will be somewhere way in the back, but it'll make Leonard Cohen sound even better than he already does.

ENAMORADO: Did Leonard Cohen make a pass at you?

LUCHA: No! He's old enough to be my father.

ENAMORADO: Those old coots are the worst. Did he?

LUCHA: No, he didn't. Don't be jealous.

ENAMORADO: Cohen. That bastard. Hell, I can sing better than he can.

LUCHA: What's the matter? (touches him) Pedro?

ENAMORADO: You're at the top of your field. You're cool, you work with cool people. Plus you make twice as much money as I do. I'm just some egghead at the Institute. Sure, the sex is great. But what happens when the smoke clears? How am I supposed to compete with Leonard Cohen?

LUCHA: Why compete at all?

ENAMORADO: 'Cause men compete! It's what we do! (slight pause) I can't help how I feel!

LUCHA: Let me make you feel better.

ENAMORADO: How?

LUCHA: I'll give you a lap-dance.

ENAMORADO: A lap-dance?

LUCHA: I'll even sing the song. It's a sexy one.

ENAMORADO: Right now?

LUCHA: No time like the present.

ENAMORADO: But -- you're wearing flannel!

LUCHA: Yeah, I'm getting ready for bed.

ENAMORADO: But that won't work.

LUCHA: Flannel?

ENAMORADO: It'll take it to another place!

LUCHA: What place?

ENAMORADO: Not a lapdance place!

LUCHA: You mean it's not sexy?

ENAMORADO: It's just that flannel will have a very non-trivial effect on the whole dance. It'll affect the interaction.

LUCHA: You're turning me down?

ENAMORADO: No! Wait! Can't you just take it off?

LUCHA: Getting naked's not a lap-dance. Anyway, it's cold.

ENAMORADO: Baby, --

LUCHA: If you wanna get technical about a lap-dance, then you shouldn't be touching me. Not unless I say so. (BEAT) Why can't flannel take lap-dancing to another dimension? Maybe a superior dimension?

ENAMORADO: Superior/inferior -- that's beside the point --

LUCHA: That first day on line for my driver's license photo, you told me that string theory was invented to describe strong interactions.

ENAMORADO: I said that?

LUCHA: I interact strongly. Particularly when I find a real connection. Because I want to feel. And at this point in my life, I want to feel BETTER.

ENAMORADO: I want to feel better too. (They embrace)

LUCHA: Hey, that's a lotta touching!

ENAMORADO: Can I have a rain-check on the lap-dance?

LUCHA: Won't it affect the interaction?

ENAMORADO: Affect this interaction.

SFX: As they fall onto the bed, CELLO returns.

SFX: The phone rings.

LUCHA: Don't you want to pick that up?

SFX: He keeps kissing. As they press into each other, BEEP, then:

GOODNIGHT: Professor Enamorado. Goodnight here. Dinner tomorrow? My place. And bring a guest. We've got connections to make.

SFX: Goodnight hangs up.

LUCHA: What happened to your strong interaction?
ENAMORADO: Gravity, my dear. Fucking gravity.

SCENE 4

SFX: The sound of bottle popping.

ENAMORADO: E-pa!
GOODNIGHT: Thanks for coming, Guys!
ENAMORADO: Nice little spread you got here. Three storeys?
GOODNIGHT: Too big for one person. My agent picked it for me.
ENAMORADO: Your agent? (to LUCHA) "Agent?"
LUCHA: Great house.
ENAMORADO: (peers over deck) Stilts, huh? I'd be afraid to be standing here when the Big One hits.
GOODNIGHT: When the Big One hits, I'd be afraid to stand just about anywhere. Where are you living?
ENAMORADO: (coughs) Apartment near campus.
GOODNIGHT: Tough neighborhood.
LUCHA: Great Mexican food. Pedro walks to work, and I can get to recording seshes with ease.
GOODNIGHT: Are you married?

LUCHA: (proudly) We're *fianceed*. Pedro's my *affiance*.
PEDRO: (less so) The other way around, actually.
GOODNIGHT: Congratulations.
LUCHA: We're happy.
GOODNIGHT: (toasts them) To love.
ENAMORADO: "Gravitation is not responsible for people falling in love." Einstein. (drinks) That was quite a lecture yesterday, lots to chew on, I was wondering, --
GOODNIGHT: Oh let's not waste the night talking shop! Lucha, you've simply got to tell me about how you met the Q of D!
ENAMORADO: Quantum Dots?

Goodnight stifles a laugh. Enamorado doesn't get the joke.

LUCHA: Disco was just about to explode. I was a teenager from North Jersey. I'd take some speed and a bottle of water and dance all night. One night there was this fabulous woman singing these kickass songs. I musta been singing along and somebody musta heard. It was like, one minute I'm on the dance floor and the next I'm onstage with two other back-up singers, going -- (sings) TOOT TOOT YEAH BEEP BEEP!
GOODNIGHT: Oh wow! TOOT TOOT YEAH BEEP BEEP! (to ENAMORADO) Donna Summer! The **Q**ueen of **D**isco!
ENAMORADO: Oh. Prosecco?
LUCHA: I love back-up. Feels like I'm INSIDE the music. My voice moves through space and wraps

itself around the singer, no matter if it's Donna or Leonard Cohen.

GOODNIGHT: You sang with Leonard Cohen?

LUCHA: I did the Cohen tour all through the Eighties. He'd come out in a Mafia suit and slicked hair, playing his Casio with one finger like a kid on a typewriter, singing from some cavern down deep inside him. He was a lot like Donna, --

ENAMORADO: Except he can't sing.

LUCHA: He sings the way he sings -- which is good enough for all the people listening.

ENAMORADO: What do I know?

GOODNIGHT: I can't believe you sang with Leonard Cohen! That's --

LUCHA: Sometimes everything comes together, fits just right. That was a sweet gig, just like being the seed inside a grape.

GOODNIGHT: (to ENAMORADO) She's FABULOUS!!

LUCHA: I'm just a girl who likes to sing harmony. (takes a long drink) I trailed off recently. New producers, new expectations. Katy Perry and Lady GaGa want a different kind of backup than I can give. They mix so much in the studio anyway, then play it back during the live shows like no one notices. But I think people do. That's why everybody still listens to all the old songs. The Old Days? It was this beautiful time -- this beautiful, beautiful time -- when we were just inspired to sing and move, and we just did it. No one told us we couldn't. It wasn't about money. Drugs, yes. And sex, of course. But not commerce.

Sure, BAD GIRLS made Donna a zillion, and I got mine. But we were just having big fun, you know? GOODNIGHT: That's just the way we were about physics. Except of course for the sex and drugs. Don't you agree, Pedro? When we were students, advanced math and quantum physics were these wonderful dream fields, and we were running through them barefoot. Not even the sky was the limit. There was this promise of beauty everywhere, if only you could learn the right way to look at things. The promise of symmetry, of everything coming together, and fitting just right, from the atomic to the galactic. We learned to analyze everything, and see things with new eyes. And it made everything more beautiful, not less. "Beauty truth//Truth Beauty" -- with not even a hint of irony. Or cynicism.

ENAMORADO: Awfully romantic.

GOODNIGHT: Well, it's not like that anymore.

ENAMORADO: It never was. Sure, we have our moments. But isn't our day-to-day mostly number crunching anyway?

GOODNIGHT: There's a difference between someone who's just trained to put numbers into a formula, and someone who's truly creating the important stuff. It's the difference between the habit of walking, and -- (to LUCHA) The skill to get up and dance.

ENAMORADO: Dancing? I remember cold nights staring at equations tacked to the wall. Maybe all the great stuff has been done. Maybe we're just playing with a string theory mirage given to us by Witten, Green, Schwarz and all those modern giants. One big daisy chain leading to Palookaville. (slight pause) Is that dancing? (downs his drink)

LUCHA: That's not dancing.

ENAMORADO: You gotta have a partner to dance.

GOODNIGHT: (more to LUCHA than ENAMORADO) Even with the sweetest partner, you dance by yourself. We Theorists are just taking a little beautiful solo right now -- but we'll be reunited soon to dance again. I think there will always be problems to solve. Maybe the dance goes on forever. We dance together, we dance alone....

ENAMORADO: Prosecco?

GOODNIGHT: We battle ourselves. To the very edge. Extend the parameters of our knowledge and our reach, our ambition and our appetite, our dreams and our disappointments. We all do it. But we all do it alone. (silence, then) TOOT TOOT YEA BEEP BEEP. (slight pause) You'll excuse me a moment?

Goodnight exits. Enamorado is silent. Then:

ENAMORADO: Okay, is he gay?

LUCHA: How should I know?

ENAMORADO: He's gay!

LUCHA: Fine, so what?

ENAMORADO: He's too interested in disco to be straight! I'm confused. He invites us out, and I'm thinking fine, it doesn't have to be a work dinner, but physics is gonna come up somehow someway. At some point in the evening, he's gonna sidle up to me and say, "So what are you working on?" With the

45

idea to scare the living daylights outa me. Because I'll have to impress him with my answer, making it sound smarter than it is -- than I am -- and it'll be our version of the showdown at the O-K Corral -- which if you read the actual accounts was an ambush and a slaughter and not at all a fair fight. So here I am all night sweating bullets preparing for the inevitable question -- and he wants to talk about DANCING?!!

LUCHA: Calm down. The night is young. You'll get your chance.

ENAMORADO: I'm just saying, what's going on here?

LUCHA: It's a gorgeous home. The moon is full. Why can't you enjoy it?

ENAMORADO: Because I don't know what comes next!!

SFX: a COYOTE HOWL.

ENAMORADO: Was that a dog?

LUCHA: Coyote I think.

ENAMORADO: I don't like this at all.

LUCHA: He's not gonna bite.

ENAMORADO: You sure?

Goodnight returns.

GOODNIGHT: BAD GIRL SAD GIRL
YOU'RE SUCH A
DIRTY BAD GIRL --

LUCHA: BEEP BEEP, UH HUH

GOODNIGHT: BAD GIRL SAD GIRL
YOU'RE SUCH A
DIRTY BAD GIRL --

LUCHA/GOODNIGHT: BEEP BEEP, UH HUH

LUCHA: You got a great voice.
GOODNIGHT: Not really.
LUCHA: Yes really! You'd be a great singer.
GOODNIGHT: I could never do that.
LUCHA: Sure you can. Anyone can.
ENAMORADO: Don't embarrass the man. Every time he opens his mouth he reveals himself.
GOODNIGHT: Do I?
ENAMORADO: Sometimes silence is the perfect response. You make a noise –

SFX: A chorus of COYOTE howls.

ENAMORADO: And you make yourself more easily located. You eliminate chance. You determine the path of your future each time you make yourself known through words, deeds, anything you do.
GOODNIGHT: True. (BEAT) So....What Are you working on?

SFX: a SMALL DOG suddenly cries out. The COYOTE howls turn to growls and grunts. As the DOG screams, --

ENAMORADO: Is that what I think it is?

GOODNIGHT: It's upsetting. But they have to eat.

ENAMORADO: Amazing! Not only do you have the Theory of Everything within your grasp--

GOODNIGHT: I don't --

ENAMORADO: -- but you can explain away the death of Poochie to the hungry jackals of the night!

LUCHA: Coyotes.

SFX: Another DOG scream.

ENAMORADO: This is awful.

SFX: One last scream. Then silence.

ENAMORADO: Did you just cross yourself?

GOODNIGHT: Nature is full of surprises. Not quite conducive to the eating of sweets. (on the run) Let me take this back inside, ...

ENAMORADO: Yeah, but what about the genuflect?

Goodnight goes. Enamorado follows.

GOODNIGHT (O.S.): I really don't need any help...!

Lucha is alone. For herself, she begins to vocalize.

LUCHA: HALLELUJAH
HALLELUJAH

SFX: Sound of her lighting up and smoking up the one-hitter.

SFX: A CELLO music played live.

SFX: Sound of her hiding the one-hitter.

Enamorado comes running out.

ENAMORADO: He's playing! Have a look! This guy is really too much for words!

SFX: The CELLO stops.

Goodnight reenters, holds the cello, lovingly.

LUCHA: Beautiful!
GOODNIGHT: You think?
LUCHA: I know.
ENAMORADO: She knows! Ah the joys of faith.
LUCHA: Faith?
ENAMORADO: Knowing without having to prove it.
LUCHA: What's to prove? It's music.
ENAMORADO: And Leonard Cohen is a great singer.
GOODNIGHT: (laughs lightly at them) A curious match!
LUCHA: Us? I guess we're an odd couple.
ENAMORADO: Complimentary. Two theories, superficially totally different in content, applied to the same physical phenomenon.

GOODNIGHT: Duality! Indeed.

ENAMORADO: Lucha and I are like two recordings. But she's analog and I'm cd.

LUCHA: Analog?

ENAMORADO: Vinyl, my dear. Classic, if a little scratched. But that only adds to the charm of the sound -- each pop has its own story. Plus the seductive album cover and great liner notes. Whereas I'm digitally encoded information, quantized, a bit over-sampled – but pure. My packaging is plastic and the liner notes are hard to read, but the sound is clean, technologically superior.

LUCHA: Superior? I thought that didn't matter.

ENAMORADO: Only technologically. It really doesn't matter how you hear it -- us, I mean.

LUCHA: But it does matter. Analog is superior to the human ear. Any musician knows that.

ENAMORADO: A slightly less than objective analysis!

LUCHA: The senses are subjective.

ENAMORADO: Scratches and all!

LUCHA: Are you saying I'm scratched?

ENAMORADO: Very attractively!

LUCHA: You really think what you do is somehow purer than what I do?

GOODNIGHT: (coming to his aid) None of us are pure, *n'est pas*?

ENAMORADO: Thank you!

LUCHA: (to ENAMORADO) Do not look down on me.

ENAMORADO: Fine. (to GOODNIGHT) Let's talk about your new model of SUSY.

GOODNIGHT: I'm skeptical.

ENAMORADO: Skeptical about your own conjectures?

GOODNIGHT: Skepticism is the default position. The burden of proof is on the believer, not the skeptic.

ENAMORADO: Burden of proof? How very Johnny Cochran of you. We both know our theories can never be true -- just true enough.

GOODNIGHT: Let's leave mine aside for another time.

ENAMORADO: So your conjectures are out of bounds, but you want to know what I'm working on?!!! Priceless, really!!!

LUCHA: (firmly) Pedro. (to GOODNIGHT) The music you played on the cello? Who wrote it?

GOODNIGHT: (relieved) No one person did. It's a realization of the equations I've been playing with.

ENAMORADO: You're saying it's science?

GOODNIGHT: Inspired by. More energy, faster vibrations, higher notes on the cello.

ENAMORADO: On the cello?!!

GOODNIGHT: On anything. My cello. (to LUCHA) Your voice.

LUCHA: Beautiful.

ENAMORADO: Ridiculous. (off LUCHA's angry react) You're telling me you're playing the music of the spheres? Please! That's a nice pick-up line at a disco bar, but don't waste my time.

LUCHA: Music is a waste of time?

ENAMORADO: Science has a point to it.

LUCHA: (after a long full silence, to GOODNIGHT) It's been a lovely evening. We're leaving now.

ENAMORADO: Lucha, --

LUCHA: Now.

GOODNIGHT: Please come again -- soon.

LUCHA: Anything's possible.

Lucha goes.

ENAMORADO: I'm in the dog house now.

GOODNIGHT: Make it up to her.

ENAMORADO: Shall we add "love doctor" to your list of accomplishments?

GOODNIGHT: Let her have faith in something.

ENAMORADO: And listen. Your music was -- it was --

GOODNIGHT: Don't make up to me. I have my faith.

ENAMORADO: You do, don't you?

Enamorado goes. Goodnight is alone under the stars. He drinks prosecco from the bottle. He starts to hum, almost despite himself:

GOODNIGHT
HALLELUJAH
HALLELUJAH
HALLELUJAH
HALLELUJAH

SFX: Coyotes begin to HOWL.

SCENE 5

SFX: Birds chirp in nearby trees.

Enamorado awakens, having slept on the couch.

ENAMORADO: "Make it up to her" -- great.

He picks up his hand-delivered newspaper at the door. Removes the plastic twine. Finds a section of the paper.

ENAMORADO: What?

Suddenly completely awake. He reads on with palpable anger as he prepares an unusually strong pot of coffee.

ENAMORADO: Oh no. (reads on) I'm dead. I'm dead.

Lucha rises from bed.

LUCHA: What?
ENAMORADO: Look!
LUCHA: (RE: the paper) Cool. I really wanna see that film --
ENAMORADO: Not that section! The Science Times!
LUCHA: Science Times section. So what? (reads) Oh wow. That's Goodnight, isn't it? Nice picture.

BRINGING SUSY HOME WITH YOU? What's that mean?

ENAMORADO: He's stolen my idea!

LUCHA: Which idea?

ENAMORADO: The one! The one I've been trying to --! (breaks off crying) The one.

LUCHA: The one that isn't finished?

ENAMORADO: It's finished now.

LUCHA: Don't give up!

ENAMORADO: *Se acabo*! He says it differently. But he's saying the same thing. And here's the beauty part. It's my idea with a twist. You see, I've been slaving -- with pride -- on something blissfully useless.

LUCHA: What do you mean, useless?

ENAMORADO: Without commercial value. The math was beautiful. It was going to show us what 95% of the universe is made of! (with hatred) But this -- this piece of work by this piece of work -- has made my idea USEFUL. He's used the same model of SUSY and applied it to everyday life! He's sold it to a company planning on building a whole new type of storage device with it. You'll be able to put endless amounts of movies, and pictures and music onto these things and access them fast. Really fast. All on something the size of a keychain!!

LUCHA: Sounds pretty useful.

ENAMORADO: He's MISUSING it. He's cheapened it. And he's making cash from it.

LUCHA: If it's a good idea, why not use it for something useful?

ENAMORADO: (ignoring her) Ah-HA! Now I get it. The agent. The amazing home in the hills. The sudden move here. This guy's gone Hollywood! Forget the Institute. Read that. He's made a deal to host a new Prime Time cable series on The Discovery Channel. He'll be the new Carl Sagan! The Oprah of Physics! Stephen Hawking played by George Clooney!

LUCHA: You always said Physics ought to have a better public face.

ENAMORADO: Not his!! It's just so dishonest! I'm being ambushed! Twenty years of my life. Everything I ever wanted to give back to Science. Every dream I ever had! It's just so goddamn dishonest!

LUCHA: Relax.

ENAMORADO: That article was written days -- weeks -- ago! And then to invite me over last night? And waste my time talking about disco?!!!

LUCHA: He didn't want to talk about physics!

ENAMORADO: He didn't have to! He was observing my behavior just before the collision.

LUCHA: What collision?

ENAMORADO: KAPOW.

(Silence)

LUCHA: His stuff sounds different from yours. You admitted that. Maybe you're overreacting, --

ENAMORADO: Am I on trial here? My ideas were stolen! I've been violated! And you blame me?

LUCHA: No. No blame.

ENAMORADO: All night -- all night -- you took his side against mine.

LUCHA: I didn't mean to.

ENAMORADO: It sure felt that way. I was gonna make you breakfast in bed. But there's no time for that now.

LUCHA: What? Where you going?

ENAMORADO: I have some dark matters to consider. SUSY needs me.

LUCHA: Does she?

SFX: CELLO music until --

Goodnight sets the cello down.

GOODNIGHT: Beautiful!

SFX: Goodnight furiously begins making notes on paper.

END ACT ONE

ENTRE ACTE

*SFX: **"Gravity" by John Mayer***

ACT TWO

<u>SCENE 1</u>

SFX: Cello music of the spheres.

Lucha enters Goodnight's deck. Finds him amidst a mass of papers.

LUCHA: (looks around) What happened?
GOODNIGHT: An original thought.

SFX: Lucha picks up an empty bottle.

LUCHA: Celebrating your article in the Science Times?
GOODNIGHT: I forgot about that.
LUCHA: Don't play with me.
GOODNIGHT: I have a lot going on in my life. Are we expecting Pedro?
LUCHA: We can expect Pedro to do something unexpected, and probably stupid.
GOODNIGHT: I'm sorry. Was it something I said?
LUCHA: Yeah. He says you stole his idea.
GOODNIGHT: I what?
LUCHA: Drop the wide-eyed innocent thing. And don't make me go into the physics of it. I'd get it all wrong.
GOODNIGHT: But I really truly don't know what he's -- you're -- talking about.

LUCHA: Get the paper and have a look.

GOODNIGHT: (changes gears) No, I think I understand. (BEAT) I feel terrible for him. Two people come to the same conclusion, continents apart. One is working in a complete vacuum, unaware of and, in so doing, somewhat wrong-footed when the other publishes the shared idea.

LUCHA: So it's his fault.

GOODNIGHT: No fault. It was unintentional --

LUCHA: He thinks otherwise.

GOODNIGHT: That's what happens when you work in a vacuum. I'm sorry.

LUCHA: What vacuum? Pedro's a tenured professor at a major university, --

GOODNIGHT: He has an excellent reputation. But he is outside certain circles of influence.

LUCHA: Such as the Science Times?

GOODNIGHT: That's public relations. Pedro knows it's meaningless.

LUCHA: The article says you've taken out a patent. That cash is not so meaningless, is it? I'm sure it'll pay for this piece of real estate, and your agent's commissions. Or are we talking something bigger than money?

GOODNIGHT: What's bigger than money? (BEAT)

LUCHA: How could two men who came to the same conclusions be so different?

GOODNIGHT: That's it in a nutshell. We're in two related, but separate, spheres. Your husband --

LUCHA: *Fiancee.*

GOODNIGHT: "*Affiance?*"

LUCHA: I get words turned around.

GOODNIGHT: Charming.

LUCHA: Pedro doesn't think so.

GOODNIGHT: You miss out on a lot of fun when you're stuck in a vacuum. I should know.

LUCHA: When you lost out to Pedro?

GOODNIGHT: To be turned away from a dream job, a chance to give my life to blissful research, to be thrown back into the dark, the wet, the work-a-day world? I missed out on years of fun. But it made me what I am today.

LUCHA: Someone who steals?

GOODNIGHT: Someone who tries not to miss out on the truly fun things in life.

LUCHA: Have fun.

GOODNIGHT: Don't go. Please.

LUCHA: I just wanted to have a look for myself. One look. Is this man for real, or not?

GOODNIGHT: Am I? For real?

LUCHA: You're a mess.

GOODNIGHT: Because I've been working!

SFX: Goodnight rifles through his papers and LPs.

GOODNIGHT: When my ideas come, they come in waves. Last night, after you left, they came through music. Usually it's the cello. But last night, -- (struggles to find the right words) It was all about the harmonies. The connection was made between us.

59

There are certain rules to all harmonic activity --
whether sung or played on strings --

SFX: Goodnight touches the cello strings.

LUCHA: Look, I don't want to know --
GOODNIGHT: -- Or in the tremors of an earthquake,
or the vibrations of the sun -- Did you know the sun
vibrates? -- Or imprinted in the sky from the earliest
violent moments of the universe. Or played out on
supernovae in galaxies beyond any poet's
imagination. Harmonies. And for some reason --
probably Freudian, probably base -- we keep
searching for the melody, the codes that stick in
memory, and resemble what we consider beautiful --
mathematical or otherwise. But you talked so lovingly
about harmonizing -- and it got me thinking about
SUSY –
LUCHA: Suzie?
GOODNIGHT: And suddenly I broke through. And it
was so clear on the other side. So amazingly clear.
LUCHA: What?
GOODNIGHT: The thing I've been missing. I don't
care what the Science Times says, or how much cash
you think I have in my bank account. I know
something has been missing. For a long, long time.
(breathes) And it's wonderful to see you. So that I can
thank you.
LUCHA: Don't.

GOODNIGHT: I keep hearing this song in my head.
(in a pleasant voice)
YOUR FAITH WAS STRONG
BUT YOU NEEDED PROOF
YOU SAW HER BATHING ON THE ROOF

LUCHA: Oh my god.

GOODNIGHT: HER BEAUTY IN THE MOONLIGHT
OVERTHREW YA

LUCHA: Stop, all right?
GOODNIGHT: What?
LUCHA: Just stop.
GOODNIGHT: There's a great phrase from the
German -- when a song gets stuck in your head and
plays over and over and you can't turn it off and
perhaps you don't want to anyway -- they say it's an
ear-worm. Well this ear-worm drove me all the way
through the night and into the morning, it was a real
slave driver! But I got something real out of it.
Something -- dare I say -- beautiful. (grabs a handful
of LPs) Who the hell could it be? And what is it trying
to tell me?
LUCHA: This is weird. I've been recording backup to
that very song.
GOODNIGHT: What's it called?
LUCHA: HALLELUJAH. I must have mentioned it at
dinner.
GOODNIGHT: I don't remember that you did.
LUCHA: But we talked about Leonard Cohen.

GOODNIGHT: Sometimes, as basketball players say, you're just in the zone. I'm just glad. I've been trying to penetrate SUSY's mysteries for years.

LUCHA: Suzie, Suzie, Suzie! Might as well be Helen of Troy. The face that launched a thousand ships!

GOODNIGHT: SUSY doesn't have a face.

LUCHA: Sure she does. She's a goddess! The more you stare into the vacuum of her eyes, the more beautiful she becomes.

GOODNIGHT: And the more we want to shed light on her dark and mysterious places. (corrects himself) *Its*. Why not anthropomorphize a bit when it comes to love?

LUCHA: Why not try to love a real person?

GOODNIGHT: Takes two. At least with physics, we can leave the truly dark matters aside for a moment -- the jealousies and envies and fears and neuroses --

LUCHA: But that's the problem. You can't. And even if you could, you won't. Maybe that's all that dark matter really is.

GOODNIGHT: What?

LUCHA: What you're afraid of. What you want.

GOODNIGHT: Fear, and desire. "You imagine what you desire; you will what you imagine; and at last you create what you will." George Bernard Shaw.

LUCHA: Great eyebrows.

GOODNIGHT: If you like them wild.

SFX: He pours her a drink. They clink glasses.

GOODNIGHT: Chin chin.

(He hums a bit, playfully, slightly seductively)

LUCHA: You really have the balls to tell me that I helped you have a breakthrough?!!
GOODNIGHT: Maybe this is yours.
LUCHA: I've had breakthroughs. In the music. Voices intertwining with a force stronger than any one of us. A force that can change the world. Yes! Change it for the better. Even if only for a moment. Bob Dylan? Aretha Franklin? Tell me they don't have the Theory of Everything nearly figured out!!?
GOODNIGHT: They very well might.
LUCHA: Don't patronize me. I've had it up to here. Pedro with his poems to Suzie. And you with your pedigree --
GOODNIGHT: Not really.
LUCHA: Yes, really! You make people feel as if what they do is not important. Not as important anyway.
GOODNIGHT: I think music is just about the most important thing in our lives.
LUCHA: More important than Suzie?
GOODNIGHT: Indubitably.
LUCHA: (a dark revelation) You are different from Pedro.
GOODNIGHT: Maybe.

(They breathe together until the patterns fall into synch)

LUCHA: I inspired you?
GOODNIGHT: One day I hope to repay the favor.

LUCHA: Oh really.

GOODNIGHT: Whatever you like. What can I get you?

LUCHA: Like what?

GOODNIGHT: An aperitif? Something to eat? (chuckles) Something stronger?

LUCHA: What do you have in mind?

GOODNIGHT: Well,.... I'm no expert. But my agent left a certain stash in the kitchen cupboard which he swears is *primo* -- (fake-coughs) Whatever that means.

LUCHA: I got my own stuff.

SFX: She breaks out her one-hitter. Knocks it against the deck to remove ash.

LUCHA: Pedro doesn't know about this. He wouldn't like it. But I deserve to have a few secrets.

GOODNIGHT: You're safe with me. (said for a laugh) We love mystery.

LUCHA: Yeah, but you don't have to be goofy about it! You don't have to murder every unexplainable moment that doesn't fit the equation you've built your entire life on!

SFX: Lucha puts the one-hitter away.

LUCHA: Not in the mood.

GOODNIGHT: What just happened?

LUCHA: Look, I don't even know you, --

GOODNIGHT: You could.

LUCHA: No! One String Theorist is enough in a girl's life! You guys take up a lotta space, you know? Everything is so important ALL THE TIME! It's exhausting. Sometimes I just wanna have a glass of wine -- or a hit – in peace. But I can't. Because I don't know you! And I don't know him either.

GOODNIGHT: You do.

LUCHA: No. Because you hide yourselves.

GOODNIGHT: I'm here.

LUCHA: Are you?

GOODNIGHT: I think you've found me out.

LUCHA: To be what?

GOODNIGHT: Real.

LUCHA: That's still to be determined. (BEAT) Everybody wants to know. What do I see in him? There's handsomer men. Apparently there's smarter men too. I wonder what he sees in me. Because Pedro doesn't listen to music. He'll suffer it. But he can't -- or won't – hear how the music can deepen, and grow richer, even as the notes fall away. For him, it just doesn't matter.

GOODNIGHT: It matters.

LUCHA: But it's broken somehow.

Again, she rises to leave.

GOODNIGHT: This ear-worm? It's still in there. Rattling around. Can't you help me?

LUCHA: How?

GOODNIGHT: Sing. If not to dislodge it, then at least to give it a little harmony.

LUCHA: Sing what?

GOODNIGHT: Something warm. See, dark matter is cold. Its particles travel slowly, when compared to light -- which is hot.

LUCHA: Are we talking particles here?

GOODNIGHT: Heat mine up.

LUCHA: I don't think so.

GOODNIGHT: We need to get rid of the worm!

LUCHA: Hey, if a song's stuck in your head, then you're the one who should sing.

GOODNIGHT: You're right! What do you suggest?

LUCHA: Something just as strong.

Goodnight grabs an LP.

GOODNIGHT: Don't go anywhere.

Exits to stereo. Lucha is alone. She hesitates. She is about to leave.

SFX: **Donna Summer** *on the stereo, and Goodnight singing along to,* **HOT STUFF**.

LUCHA: You gotta be kidding me.

Goodnight reenters, dancing.

GOODNIGHT:
SITTING HERE EATING MY HEART OUT
WAITING
WAITING FOR SOME LOVER TO CALL

DIALED ABOUT A THOUSAND NUMBERS
LATELY
ALMOST RANG THE PHONE OFF THE WALL
LOOKING FOR SOME HOT STUFF --

LUCHA: Are you crazy?

GOODNIGHT:
I WANT SOME HOT STUFF
BABY THIS EVENING

LUCHA: No way!

She moves away from him. He follows, dancing.

LUCHA: Are you giving me a lap-dance?
GOODNIGHT: I want to give you a Eureka moment.
LUCHA: No thanks!

Goodnight dances. It's funny, a little sexy, very goofy. As much as Lucha wants to remain severe, he wears her defenses down.

GOODNIGHT: You're not gonna sing, are ya?
LUCHA: You can't afford me. (as he dances) Stop!

SFX: Sound of the elastic snap of a man's underwear.

GOODNIGHT: Finally!

Exhausted, he stops, sits beside her.

GOODNIGHT: One dollar? That's all I'm good for?
Oh God! I'm out of shape.
LUCHA: So you do this for money, huh?
GOODNIGHT: I do it for love. But I take cash.
LUCHA: You're a goofball!
GOODNIGHT: You know me!

He attempts a kiss.

LUCHA: Nice try.
GOODNIGHT: This is not just a come-on.
LUCHA: You're not looking for some hot stuff?
GOODNIGHT: I'm always looking but seldom
finding.
LUCHA: Like Pedro with Suzie.
GOODNIGHT: Like all of us with SUSY.
LUCHA: But Pedro most of all.
GOODNIGHT: You're really committed to him?
Neuroses and all?
LUCHA: I love him. (pause) How was this display
supposed to bring me to a Eureka moment?
GOODNIGHT: Listen to yourself.
LUCHA: Huh?
GOODNIGHT: "I love him!"
LUCHA: But I already knew that!
GOODNIGHT: Breakthroughs don't have to be new!
You break through the dark stuff to connect to the
stuff you already know.
LUCHA: (altered) Listen, uh -- something just --
GOODNIGHT: You gotta go.

LUCHA: Yes.

GOODNIGHT: My love to Pedro.

LUCHA: The molasses sea? I think that's me. I can barely understand anything you guys say. Yet something always sticks. The words you use, the phrases to describe your theories, sometimes I feel like I could almost sing them. Dark matter? That thing that we know is there, but don't know what it is? I know that too. I've felt it a zillion times in my business. When the voice cracks, tears -- when technique falls away and you're left unmasked, alone, with nothing to fall back on that you can see or know. Only feeling. Only fear. Secrets. Desire. Who we really are.

She exits. Returns.

LUCHA: This meeting never happened.

Exits. Shuts the stereo off.

SCENE 2

Enamorado enters, rubs his neck and unshaven cheek. He kicks off his shoes. Yawns, stretches his back. Still stretching and yawning, he grabs a bag of cookies. Lucha enters.

LUCHA: Don't eat those.

ENAMORADO: I'm ravenous.

LUCHA: I'll take you out.

ENAMORADO: I just took off my shoes.

LUCHA: Fine. Eat the bag while you're at it.

ENAMORADO: Where were you?

LUCHA: Testing a theory.

ENAMORADO: Oh yeah? I was tearing one down.

LUCHA: You didn't do anything stupid, did you?

ENAMORADO: On the contrary. I was on deadline. So I finished my paper.

LUCHA: Your paper? The paper? That's AMAZING!

ENAMORADO: It's what it is.

LUCHA: You gotta let me take you out! We need champagne.

ENAMORADO: Pour me a glass of milk. These cookies are dry as sand.

LUCHA: Wheat-less. Watching my figure.

ENAMORADO: I'm watching it right now.

LUCHA: Shall we celebrate? Like that?

ENAMORADO: Cookies first.

LUCHA: Why did your paper tear down a theory? I thought you were building something wonderful and new, --

ENAMORADO: Destroy to create. Create to destroy. (munches) I almost went to Goodnight's to confront him face to face.

LUCHA: Today?

ENAMORADO: No time like the present. But what would that prove? The gorilla outweighs me by twenty pounds. Probably knows *Krav Maga* or *Jiu Jitsu* anyway. So I turned around and went back to my office. I kept trying to tell myself to calm down, that this can happen, that maybe just maybe Goodnight and I happened down the same dark alley of string theory and he happened to get there a step ahead. But it didn't wash. I pulled out my halfwritten paper, and it looked so sad, so dingy, so completely second-rate. I could see it unraveling in front of me on the page -- all my calculations halfbaked, all my bold conjectures falling flat. How could I ever have thought this new idea could work? Gimme a break! I started to tear it apart. And then a weird thing happened. In the unraveling, parts of the paper started to get stronger. With blood on my hands from the carnage of my leaky red pen, I started to see something new. Something wonderful. And the most wonderful part was how it refuted my distinguished colleague's findings discussed in the Science Times! A complete evisceration. (slight pause) I've never finished a paper so fast. Or felt so good about it.

LUCHA: That's...great. I guess.

ENAMORADO: I'm going to take him down. He made some stupid mistakes, and so did I. But I see them now and he doesn't! He's going down! But I gotta do it fast. I gotta come packing. One shot through the heart. Let's hope he has one. (munches) He must think I'm a chump.

LUCHA: No. He doesn't.

ENAMORADO: Where were you again?

LUCHA: I was -- (stops, starts) I don't like to lie to you.

ENAMORADO: Good. Don't.

LUCHA: Don't ask me.

ENAMORADO: Where were you?

LUCHA: It wasn't like that, it was --

ENAMORADO: Where?

LUCHA: You know where.

ENAMORADO: *Hijo de puta*! Why?

LUCHA: It was an experiment.

ENAMORADO: What does that mean?

LUCHA: I wanted to see him without you there. Your presence alters the interaction.

ENAMORADO: A control? How scientific of you! So you're testing the structure of the relationship, then?

LUCHA: Whose?

ENAMORADO: Ours, of course.

LUCHA: I was thinking more your relationship to Goodnight.

ENAMORADO: I have none.

LUCHA: Of course you do! You think about him night and day!

ENAMORADO: Don't joust with me. I'm in a dangerous mood. And I'm getting good at unraveling things. So? Did the structure survive? (slight pause) Your silence speaks universes.

LUCHA: Goodnight didn't mean to hurt you. But now I can see that you mean to hurt him.

ENAMORADO: Why are you taking his side? Are you in love with this guy?

LUCHA: I'm in love with THIS guy! But I don't like you. Not this dark energy.

ENAMORADO: Dark *Matter*.

LUCHA: You're tearing the flesh off your own ideas just to inflict pain on him. But it hurts me too.
ENAMORADO: Why?
LUCHA: Because I had faith in you!
ENAMORADO: "Had?" Wow. In one fell swoop he steals my idea and my girl. He suckered you into talking about yourself and your songs -- all that stuff from your glorious PAST. Did you kiss him?
LUCHA: You said he was gay!
ENAMORADO: You did, didn't you? He seduced you away from me. And I'm gonna get him for that.
LUCHA: I want no part of it.
ENAMORADO: It doesn't matter what you want.

SFX: She removes a suitcase from under the bed. Starts to pack.

ENAMORADO: What are you doing?
LUCHA: Do you think you're the only one who got your heart broken? The out-and-out robberies of songs, of voices! Voices recorded and rerecorded till they lose their identity, then mixed into someone else's track. The unbelievable injustice every time you hear yourself on the radio, every time, and no one knows but you who's really singing. I'm not even talking about the loss of revenue. But to lose your own voice, --
ENAMORADO: That happened to you?
LUCHA: That and a lot more.

(Silence)

ENAMORADO: All the more reason.
LUCHA: For what?
ENAMORADO: Revenge.
LUCHA: No!

SFX: *She resumes packing.*

ENAMORADO: Don't be so emotional.
LUCHA: I've had enough drama in my life, I didn't think you were that kind of guy.
ENAMORADO: What kind of guy?
LUCHA: A DUMB kinda guy!
ENAMORADO: I am not dumb!
LUCHA: I was. But no more.

SFX: *She zips up the suitcase.*

ENAMORADO: Baby! Come on. Look. Wait! WAIT!! I'll go. I gotta go anyway.
LUCHA: Where?
ENAMORADO: I told you. I gotta go take somebody down.
LUCHA: You're a thug!
ENAMORADO: Don't call me that! I'm a string theorist!
LUCHA: You're a bully!
ENAMORADO: I'm not! I've spent my life trying to get away from bullies and thugs. Not too many string theorists come from my tenement block! I'm a fast runner. I learned that from being chased on a daily basis. Then when I finally wrote my ticket outta

Dodge, I found myself getting bullied in academia. And even now, with a professorship and on the verge of great things, here I am getting pushed around! Chased outa my own field. I'm the one getting bullied! And yeah, maybe I did learn a couple dirty punches along the way, and maybe I've thrown a couple and I'm gonna throw a couple more if some egghead gets in my way. But don't you ever call me a thug! DO YOU HEAR ME?

SFX: She opens the door to leave.

ENAMORADO: I love you.
LUCHA: No you don't. I thought you were in love with Suzie. But you don't care about her either. Who do you love?
ENAMORADO: I love honesty.
LUCHA: Make love to honesty, then. Goodbye, Pedro.
ENAMORADO: And for the record? Superpartners have no superpowers. They're absolutely nothing like **"The Incredibles."**
LUCHA: Indeed.

She leaves. He sits alone against the wall. Finally:

ENAMORADO:
BAD GIRL SAD GIRL YOU'RE SUCH A
DIRTY BAD GIRL....

SFX: He mumbles figures in his head, counting with his fingers against the wall, working something out with his entire being.

ENAMORADO: TOOT TOOT, YEAH BEEP BEEP....

SCENE 3

Six weeks later.

SFX: of a buzzing crowd packed into a small amphitheater.

SFX: CAMERAS overhead and at the sides. A LIVE TAPING of Goodnight's Cable TV program on physics. SOUNDS of a TV CREW, DIRECTOR, CAMERAMEN, GRIPS, ETC.

Goodnight onstage, with a blackboard.

SFX: the chalk's unnerving squeak as he does rapid equations.

GOODNIGHT: So, 83% of the matter in the universe is in a form unknown to us! And 73% of all the mass-energy in the universe is unknown to us, that 73% being dark energy. That makes a total of almost 96% of our universe being made of unknown stuff. And yet, as you can see, we're getting closer to knowing. Consider these equations -- to quote a Korean phrase -- the skin of the watermelon. We theorists strive to understand the mysteries of Dark Matter. It's not always visible to us, it emits no radiation that we can observe. Yet it matters. It matters deeply in all our lives -- yours and mine, and those to come.

SFX: APPLAUSE

SFX: Laughter from a single man in the dark.

GOODNIGHT: Thanks to the Griffith Park Observatory for the use of the planetarium for this live television event. Till next week, I'm Aaron Good --

SFX: More laughter, louder now.

GOODNIGHT: Perhaps you can let us in on the joke?

Enamorado emerges from the audience.

GOODNIGHT: Professor Enamorado! Frivolities aside, our work is far too important to be laughed at.
ENAMORADO: I'm only laughing at yours.
GOODNIGHT: Please. Don't do something rash, --
ENAMORADO: The watermelon is rotten.
GOODNIGHT: How did you arrive at that conclusion?
ENAMORADO: Because it was my idea first.

SFX: Rustling nervousness from the audience.

GOODNIGHT: Nonsense. (pleading) We can discuss this another time.

ENAMORADO: There is no other time. Your idea about SUSY doesn't work, Pal. *No sirve!* Your billion dollar computer toy won't work.
GOODNIGHT: (looking around for help) This isn't going out live, is it?
ENAMORADO: Your mistake begins on the first line of the equations.
GOODNIGHT: How would you know?
ENAMORADO: Because I made the same mistake. I've had a lot more free time lately. Six weeks to think. No one pulling me away from my work. A lot of catching up. (turns cold) Whatever. You -- we -- missed a crucial family of quantum corrections --

Enamorado joins Goodnight onstage.

GOODNIGHT: No, that's not right. I checked the quantum corrections several times, --
ENAMORADO: I couldn't see it either. But look with new eyes, and you see things for what they are.
GOODNIGHT: There is an infinite set of corrections, you'd have to handle all of them -- you'd have to be God -- to see that!
ENAMORADO: I can sum it up nicely. I've been working on it pretty much night and day.

Enamorado takes over the stage. Emptiness except for an old-fashioned whiteboard at the back. Enamorado picks up a marker. He writes two equations on the board.

Silence.

SCENE 4

Pedro enters a urinal. As he pees, Goodnight rushes in.
Silence as he stares. Pedro squirms as he is unable to pee.

GOODNIGHT: (finally) That was an ambush.
ENAMORADO: It was a showdown.
GOODNIGHT: It was a mugging. How was I – as a
scientist – supposed to defend myself? (pause) Now
what?

Pedro laughs, but continues to squirm.

ENAMORADO: Are you gonna pee? If not, could you
please leave me in peace?
GOODNIGHT: Peace is pretty much out of the
question. How can you just throw away all that
work? All your dreams?
ENAMORADO: My dreams?
GOODNIGHT: My theory gets shot down, so does
yours.
ENAMORADO: Ah-HA!

SFX: Enamorado zips up.

ENAMORADO: Then you do know my work.
GOODNIGHT: I did not steal from you!
ENAMORADO: Then how do you know my theory?
My mistakes?
GOODNIGHT: I don't. *My* theory --
ENAMORADO: The one you pimped?

GOODNIGHT: The one you destroyed out there. *Our* theory. Set aflame. You'd cut off your nose to spite your face.

ENAMORADO: You'd rather keep your Pinocchio nose? Gets bigger with every lie.

GOODNIGHT: I don't lie. And this peacock show of machismo is very unbecoming.

ENAMORADO: Wimp!

GOODNIGHT: Don't bully me, Enamorado.

ENAMORADO: Can't you take it?

GOODNIGHT: This isn't the South Bronx.

ENAMORADO: Don't go there! You don't know a thing about the Bronx.

GOODNIGHT: And from your thuggish actions, you obviously know too much.

ENAMORADO: Where I come from, liars get a foot up their lying asses!

GOODNIGHT: You can't talk to me that way, Sir.

ENAMORADO: Gravity's a bitch, ain't it Goodnight? (waits for a response) What are you gonna do, cry?

GOODNIGHT: Have you no soul?

ENAMORADO: Excuse me?

GOODNIGHT: Where's your heart, Pedro?

ENAMORADO: Hardly scientific, are ya Goodnight?

GOODNIGHT: Where's your love?

ENAMORADO: I....I think I lost it somewhere.

GOODNIGHT: Then how do you expect to do anything -- anything at all -- till you get it back?

ENAMORADO: She left me.

GOODNIGHT: Lucha?

ENAMORADO: SUSY. My boyhood crush. My unending hard-on. My beautiful Suzie. I thought she left me for you. Now she's broken both our hearts.

GOODNIGHT: *La Belle Dame Sans Merci.*

ENAMORADO: I don't speak French.

GOODNIGHT: "I met a lady in the meads, Full Beautiful -- a faery's child,
Her hair was long, her foot was light,
And her eyes were wild."

ENAMORADO: Wild as hell.

GOODNIGHT: "And there she lulled me asleep,
And there I dream'd -- ah! woe betide!
The latest dream I ever dream'd
On the cold hill's side."

ENAMORADO: Cold as shit.

GOODNIGHT: "I saw pale kings and princes too,
Pale warriors, death-pale were they all:
They cried, "La belle Dame sans Merci
Hath thee in thrall!"

ENAMORADO: I'm lost. She left me.

GOODNIGHT: SUSY?

ENAMORADO: Lucha!

Pedro breaks down crying.

ENAMORADO: She didn't want me to do this. But I just kept going and going.

GOODNIGHT: Get up, Enamorado. Someone's liable to come in any second. The last thing String Theory needs is a tabloid story about two proponents weeping in a urinal! How will we explain ourselves?

ENAMORADO: We're human! "If you prick us, do we not bleed?" See, I read some English Lit in my time too! (slight pause) Ohhh. I'm gonna be sick. Oh God I'm a fool! I've wrecked everything!

GOODNIGHT: Do you know where Lucha is?

ENAMORADO: No. *Lucha* means struggle, and I've been struggling all my life. I have nothing to give her. Yeah, we were great in the sack. My attractiveness was the whole Professor chic, the sexiness of knowing something arcane, difficult, special. Now I know nothing, I'm like any other schlub on the beginners slope. Physics 101. That's not sexy.

GOODNIGHT: There's nothing sexier than the beginning of a love affair. Especially if it's the love of your life. (BEAT) Sorry.

ENAMORADO: Sorry?

GOODNIGHT: I've been doing five things all at once. You've been doing one thing for twenty years. Sorry we ended up at the same place, at the wrong time.

ENAMORADO: Tortoise and the Hare. Either way we end up in the soup. Heartbreak Soup. (BEAT) Sorry for all that stuff I said.

GOODNIGHT: Sorry for what I've done too.

ENAMORADO: What'd you do?

GOODNIGHT: (coughs) Let's not dwell. All in the past! (changing gears) So you've gone over my theory with a fine-toothed comb?

ENAMORADO: Every computation I could lay my hands on.

GOODNIGHT: And you've found its weakness.

ENAMORADO: You saw me out there.

GOODNIGHT: What about its strength?

ENAMORADO: Well, there's a lot to choose from.

GOODNIGHT: Indeed?

ENAMORADO: You know yourself. The sophistication of the idea is intoxicating.

GOODNIGHT: Then who's to say we can't begin again? There's money -- **lots of money** -- to research its efficacy. Yes, you've bashed in sections of its hull for all the world to see. But what if the watermelon's center somehow – despite all -- remained sweet?

ENAMORADO: What does that mean?

GOODNIGHT: I don't know. What does that mean? We won't know unless we look – together. (BEAT) Shake on it?

ENAMORADO: Lemme wash my hands.

GOODNIGHT: Neither of us is clean, Pedro.

ENAMORADO: Then let's start now.

GOODNIGHT: Now? It's late!

ENAMORADO: So? I'll come up to your place.

GOODNIGHT: Give me a head start.

Goodnight exits ahead of Enamorado.

SCENE 5

Lucha smokes on Goodnight's deck.

LUCHA: (to herself)
SHE TIED YOU
TO A KITCHEN CHAIR
SHE BROKE YOUR THRONE

83

AND SHE CUT YOUR HAIR
AND FROM YOUR LIPS SHE DREW THE
HALLELUJAH

Goodnight enters on the run. They embrace.

LUCHA: You're on fire.
GOODNIGHT: (pulling back slightly) Lucha, --
LUCHA: You want a puff? (watches him) Take off
your coat and stay awhile.
GOODNIGHT: Something's come up.

She sets the one-hitter on the railing.

LUCHA: So?
GOODNIGHT: Something big, unforeseen. I have to
get to work. And you have to go away for awhile. Not
forever. I'm sorry. It's just that something....
LUCHA: Came up? Okay.
GOODNIGHT: You don't mind?
LUCHA: No strings, right?
GOODNIGHT: It's all strings, actually.
LUCHA: You're all right?
GOODNIGHT: I'm great! (struggles to explain) I just
want you to know. These last six weeks have been a
dream to me. I was in a rut, unable to see, unable to
be, --
LUCHA: You're rhyming now? What are you, a poet?
GOODNIGHT: I'm trying to thank you. And Pedro.
LUCHA: A funny way to thank Pedro.

GOODNIGHT: Sorry, but I kind of need you to go now.
LUCHA: Oh. Sure. (BEAT) And for the record? Us? Booty call.

Goodnight goes through his LPs.

LUCHA: What's this?

SFX: She opens it.

LUCHA: **Various Positions**.
GOODNIGHT: Leonard Cohen.
LUCHA: Talk about a theory of everything.

He starts to hum, then to sing:

GOODNIGHT: HALLELUJAH
HALLELUJAH

GOODNIGHT/LUCHA: HALLELUJAH

LUCHA: (stops) The song is what it is. It's the voice that makes it sticky. That makes it sweet. That makes it more.
GOODNIGHT: Indeed.

She leaves.

He continues to hum the Leonard Cohen song as he rolls on a blackboard on wheels.

SCENE 6

Goodnight's deck, late night. Blackboard well-used with equations erased and written over. Enamorado and Goodnight together.

ENAMORADO: No, that's clearly dodgy.
GOODNIGHT: That's because it's not done yet!

SFX: Enamorado writes furiously.

GOODNIGHT: No. You've over-egged the pudding.
ENAMORADO: Exactly my intention. I like eggs. And as my uncle often said, (heavily accented) "The proof is in the poodDING!"
GOODNIGHT: It's time to sleep.
ENAMORADO: Who have you got waiting for you but some hungry coyotes? They'll be coming around for you next.
GOODNIGHT: Tomorrow, Casanova. It's been quite a night.
ENAMORADO: If we're going to finish my paper it's got to be fast and it has to be good.
GOODNIGHT: Your paper? Our paper.
ENAMORADO: Our paper.
GOODNIGHT: What if it's no good?
ENAMORADO: Our paper?
GOODNIGHT: What if it's A Theory of Nothing? If we've wasted our lives?
ENAMORADO: We wouldn't have been the first.

GOODNIGHT: There's no apple falling on anyone's head, Pedro. Not this time.
ENAMORADO: Says you.
GOODNIGHT: The fatal law of gravity: when you're down, everything falls down on you.
ENAMORADO: But we're not dead yet.

Shared silence. Enamorado picks up the marker, starts to write equations.

ENAMORADO: Now, if we write the mass differences of the pairs of particles in this way, then --

Lucha enters, in long coat over her flannels. The Leonard Cohen LP under her arm. As long a silence as will hold.

LUCHA: Then...what?
ENAMORADO: Then they each get sticky.
GOODNIGHT: Apart, and together.
LUCHA: (stares at each of them) Sticky.
GOODNIGHT: Very sticky.
ENAMORADO: What are you doing here?

Lucha picks up her one-hitter.

LUCHA: (looking from one to the other) Something came up.
ENAMORADO: What, exactly?
LUCHA: A breakthrough of sorts.
GOODNIGHT: I'll leave you two, --
LUCHA: It started as a breakdown.

ENAMORADO: Lucha, -- (clears throat) What are you doing *here*?

LUCHA: I could be asking you the same question.

ENAMORADO: It is a bit baffling.

LUCHA: You never called me. But your friend here called nearly every day... *and* night.

ENAMORADO: Really?

SFX: Enamorado breaks the CHALK in his hand.

LUCHA: (to ENAMORADO) We hooked up to get back at you. (to GOODNIGHT) Didn't we?

GOODNIGHT: There might be that hidden dimension.

Goodnight begins erasing equations. Lucha turns to go.

ENAMORADO: Eureka. (to LUCHA) Hold on. (to GOODNIGHT) Can I have a moment?

GOODNIGHT: Take more than one.

Goodnight exits quickly.

LUCHA: Your eyebrows are a mess.

ENAMORADO: You're wearing flannels.

LUCHA: I just got out of bed. Look, I know what you're thinking, --

ENAMORADO: I'm not thinking.

LUCHA: That's good.

ENAMORADO: I'm feeling. It's the presence of unobserved matter.

He touches her.

LUCHA: Don't do that.
ENAMORADO: Lucha. We can handle a little mess.
LUCHA: A little?
ENAMORADO: This mess is our life. SUSY is broken.
LUCHA: Don't talk about Suzie –
ENAMORADO: We are Suzie. We've proved it. We
are it. (BEAT) And for that, we deserve a prize.
LUCHA: A prize? Me or you?
ENAMORADO: Me first.
LUCHA: Like a Nobel?
ENAMORADO: Something bigger. Maybe you
wanna give me that lap-dance?
LUCHA: You gotta be kidding.
ENAMORADO: Hey, I'm calling in a rain-check here!
LUCHA: No!
ENAMORADO: All right then. You asked for it.

Enamorado starts to dance. A Latino without rhythm, but he tries.

LUCHA: Don't do that, okay?

ENAMORADO: (sings, not well)
AND EVEN THOUGH IT ALL WENT WRONG
I'LL STAND BEFORE THE LORD OF SONG
WITH NOTHING ON MY TONGUE BUT
HALLELUJAH

LUCHA: Wait, --

ENAMORADO: We don't have time to wait.

He kisses her.

LUCHA: Why that song?
ENAMORADO: All night long, Goodnight has been humming it incessantly. Like it will help him get somewhere.
LUCHA: Did it?
ENAMORADO: I can only speak for myself.

Enamorado hums HALLELUJAH.

Lucha separates herself.

LUCHA: If we're Suzie – if we are broken – then why should we come back together at all?
ENAMORADO: Because we are superpartners. With superpowers!
LUCHA: If we ever had the guts to use them. (highly unsure) Superpowers?
ENAMORADO: KAPOW! And if we can just learn how this whole thing works together,... then maybe we can finally get a handle on the universe.

Goodnight reappears, walks to the blackboard and begins working steadily on equations.

LUCHA: Or not.

Lucha looks out at the darkness.

GOODNIGHT: Eureka.

Enamorado stands mid-way between them, holding his breath.

END OF PLAY

LAWS OF SYMPATHY

BY

OLIVER MAYER

LAWS OF SYMPATHY

The world premiere occurred at Studio/Stage, Los Angeles, CA on February 28, 2009, produced by Playwrights Arena, directed by Jon Lawrence Rivera.

Cast:

Mother Anita Dashiell

Jaspora Diarra Kilpatrick

Mohammed Joshua Wolf Coleman

Bettye Celeste Den

Gerald Will Dixon

Southern Lady, Glenna, Ida Lou Barbara Lee Bragg

Time/Place: The mid 2000s/Atlanta, GA.

Produced by Playwrights Arena, and directed by Jon Lawrence Rivera

set design by John H. Binkley
lighting design by Jeremy Pivnick
sound design by Dennis Yen
costume design by Mylette Nora
casting director/associate producer Raul Clayton Staggs
associate producer Diane Levine

*IN THE SEMI-DARK, THE CAST SINGS BEN
HARPER'S "WHEN SHE BELIEVES."*
CAST OH THE GOOD LORD IS SUCH A GOOD
LORD WITH SUCH A GOOD MOTHER TOO THEY
HAVE BLESSED ME THEY HAVE BLESSED ME IN
THE GOOD GRACES OF YOU....

SCENE 1

A low-rent Atlanta/Decatur apartment.

INDOORS, -

*JASPORA stares at the toilet. She flushes. Then she flushes
again. Twenty, tall, beautiful and very dark. Bright-colored
well-worn robes cover her head and body.*

CAST: I HAVE HEARD A HUNDRED VIOLINS
CRYING AND I HAVE SEEN A HUNDRED WHITE
DOVES FLYING

*MOTHER, 40, shorter and wider. Over her robes she
wears a T-shirt of a prominent aid organization. She sits in
front of a TV. SOUND of several (in)famous reality TV
themes, "Survivor" in particular.*

CAST: BUT NOTHING IS AS BEAUTIFUL AS
WHEN SHE BELIEVES WHEN SHE BELIEVES
WHEN SHE BELIEVES WHEN SHE BELIEVES
WHEN SHE BELIEVES WHEN SHE BELIEVES....

The toilet flushes again.

OUTDOORS, -

MOHAMMED CHANG stands, late 30s. A large paper bag at his feet. BETTY DUBUISSON smokes. Pretty, nervous, late 20s.

MOHAMMED: Comfy.
BETTY: Comfier than a civil war in Somalia, yeah. Than flies and triple digit temperatures and dust storms and refugee camps and poisonous spiders and scorpions and troughs to shit in and parasites in the water and rape and slavery and death squads and Sudanese genocide -
MOHAMMED: Yes, Atlanta is comfier. Of course, you haven't been here in the summer.

They stand on a cement landing outside the apartment.

Jaspora flushes the toilet.

BETTY: If she flushes that toilet again, I'm calling the paramedics.
MOHAMMED: Relax. It's not diarrhea.
BETTY: What else I could have done? I turned on the TV, stocked the fridge with soda, turned down the bedspread.
MOHAMMED: (with irony) What more is there?

Betty tries to peak through the keyhole.

BETTY: What if they forget? If they go native and decide to start a fire in the middle of the living room, if they try to dig a trough – we're on the second floor!
MOHAMMED: They won't forget.
BETTY: They're like children! They'll never make it in the real world!!

Betty steps on her cigarette butt, lights another.

MOHAMMED: They will. The Hmong did. The Lost Boys of Sudan. Now it's their turn.
BETTY: Every amenity could blow up in their faces -- microwave, furnace, washer/dryer -- each one a potential land mine, a weapon of mass destruction.
MOHAMMED: Relax, Betty.
BETTY: How can we assume they can open a door just because it has a doorknob?
MOHAMMED: They'll open it. Eventually.
BETTY: How did you get to be so cool?
MOHAMMED: You've been to a foreign country?
BETTY: France.
MOHAMMED: You speak French?
BETTY: Retarded French.
MOHAMMED Remember your first day?
BETTY: In Paris? They were so mean! And have you ever tried using Paris pay phones? Their toilets? Those two footprints and the hole? Yuck!
MOHAMMED: What did you do?
BETTY: When I got back to my hotel room I closed the curtains and cried. I didn't come out till - (realizes) Oh. Right. Is that what's going on in there?

MOHAMMED : They've been through an entire process of acculturation. Maybe it'll stick; maybe it won't. They'll survive either way. Gimme.

Takes her cigarette, tokes once, then crushes it.

BETTY: Hey!
MOHAMMED: "Tobacco is a dirty weed. I like it. But ill habits gather by unseen degrees -- as brooks make rivers, rivers run to seas."
BETTY: You're a strange dude.
MOHAMMED: I was like them. But that's another story.

Betty spruces herself up the best she can.

BETTY: I hate first meetings. If they don't like me, we'll still have to pretend to get along for the next four months!
MOHAMMED: By law they get four months of government assistance. But they only get us for two weeks. So you're off the hook in 14 days. (checks watch) Actually, 13 days and 22-some-odd hours.
BETTY: Two weeks? That's nothing! (checks the keyhole again) What if they're dead from monoxide poisoning? If they thought the bleach was 7UP? What if they're already dead?
MOHAMMED: You can't live their life for them. You wouldn't want to. But we'll go in.
BETTY: You're pretty good at this.
MOHAMMED: This is my life.

He smiles, sadly.

They go in.

BETTY: Knock-knock!

Mother sits expressionless. Survivor theme on TV.

BETTY: (cont'd) Hello, Missus Abdekadir. I'm Betty!
(no reaction)
MOHAMMED: Mohammed. (MOTHER looks up) *A*
salaam alaykum.
MOTHER *Alaykum a salaam.*
BETTY : (sits with her) We at Refugee Resettlement
are so thrilled to have you here. (gets up nervously)
Are you hungry? We have chicken and beef and
beans and cabbage and canned soup and corn and -
(trails off) Do you like this show? It's called
"Survivor." I can program other reality shows, it's not
hard, - (takes the remote) There's a bunch of juicy
ones, *Dancing With The Stars* and *Extreme Makeover*
and *The Biggest Loser* - Through it all Mother smiles a
general, distant smile.
MOHAMMED: She doesn't know how to change
channels.
BETTY: What? Oh.

Mohammed winks. Slowly, as with a child, Bettye
demonstrates the channel changer.

BETTY (cont'd): This is ON. This is OFF. See?

Betty enters kitchen area.

BETTY: (cont'd) This is your kitchen! Your fridge. Your sink. Your garbage disposal – don't put your hand in there! Your microwave -- gets mighty hot! Don't burn your tongue when you make tea! Your dishwasher, - (examines it) Hey! It doesn't work! Goshdarnit! What the heck is wrong with this thing -- ?

MOHAMMED: It doesn't matter.

BETTY: But it's on the fritz! They're supposed to have all the amenities! Geez!

MOHAMMED: Betty. They can feel your nervousness.

BETTY: Anyone with a pulse could. I'm catching something. My back hurts. And I have a splitting headache.

MOHAMMED: Sympathy.

BETTY: What?

MOHAMMED: Laws of sympathy. (an explanation) I have a cold and you sneeze.

BETTY: You mean I'm crazy.

MOHAMMED: Quite the opposite. We're connected. Like produces like. If you feel, --

Jaspora enters. She is so beautiful that everyone stops.

JASPORA: Toilet? FanTAStic.

Jaspora returns to the bathroom. Silence in her wake.

BETTY: How do you feel?
MOHAMMED: Very sympathetic.

Mohammed gives Jaspora the paper bag. Jaspora removes a good quality terri-cloth robe.

Mohammed bows slightly.

Mother changes the channel. **Reality Show Theme** *gives way to:*

CAST: HOW GOOD IT MUST FEEL TO BE SO YOUNG AND FREE AND A SONG THAT PLEASES A QUEEN WILL ALWAYS PLEASE ME....

SCENE 2

LIVE MUSIC gives way to generic white noise recorded pop music.

INDOORS, -

A SOUTHERN MINI-MART. Crammed with stuff, very regional. A SOUTHERN LADY presides at the till -- quite white.

The front door is just closing, tiny cowbell above.

SOUTHERN LADY: Y'all come back now, y'hear?

Jaspora and Mother enter. Now both wear T-shirts over their robes. Mother carries a purse firmly, weapon-like. Southern Lady smiles benignly, unfazed by their different appearance.

SOUTHERN LADY: (to JASPORA) Hi, Sweetie.

Jaspora and Mother examine of the shelves. At first it"s like going to a record store and being unable to focus. But curiosity begins to win out as they examine brillo pads, party favors, Mister Pibb, Rice Krispies, and the million other notables of our culture.

SOUTHERN LADY: (cont'd) Let me know if you need some help now! The Krispy Kremes are fresh and hot!

Southern Lady leans out from her perch. She smiles, but she also checks the mirror to see if they're stealing.

OUTDOORS, -

BETTY: Krispy Kremes.
MOHAMMED: Addictive. But they go straight here. (grabs his belly)
BETTY: Ah, cool out. You need something to grab hold of when you get cuddly.
MOHAMMED: Cuddly?
BETTY: (winks, lights a cigarette) Can't we go in?
MOHAMMED: They survived the refugee camps at Dadaab and Kakuma, they should be able to

penetrate the mysteries of the AM/PM without a rescue party.

Mohammed stares at a row of gumball machines.

BETTY: (fishes in her bag) Want some gum?
MOHAMMED: No thanks.
BETTY: Then what're you looking at?
MOHAMMED: My first and only vice.
BETTY: You only have one?
MOHAMMED: Only one I care to divulge. (sighs) I remember my first time.
BETTY: First time what? Crush? Sex? Break-up?
MOHAMMED: First Homie.
BETTY: (flummoxed) Like -- homie?

Mohammed pulls out two quarters. Turns the crank. Pulls out a plastic egg.

BETTY: (cont'd) That's weird!

Mohammed opens the container. Pulls out a figurine.

MOHAMMED: Here.
BETTY: This little toy thingie? (examines it) Cool.
MOHAMMED: I got the entire collection.
BETTY: How many?
MOHAMMED: 104 and counting.
BETTY: And I thought these machines were for gumballs! Silly me. Fifty cents, huh?

She searches her pockets for change. Mohammed winks.

MOHAMMED: I avoided most all drugs, but I couldn't escape the sultry ways of these urban figurines. (presents it to her) For you.
BETTY: Wow. My first Homie! It's all downhill from here. (examines it) What's the attraction?
MOHAMMED: That's always the question, isn't it?

They enter. The COWBELL rings.

SOUTHERN LADY: Hi. Krispy Kremes are fresh -
BETTY: (RE: MOHAMMED) Tell Fatty.

Jaspora and Mother have selected a very few items. Extremely frugal, modest, fresh things. Rice, mangoes, onions.

BETTY: (cont'd) That's all?
JASPORA: What if they run out?
SOUTHERN LADY: That'll be the day.
MOHAMMED: They're not going to run out. You don't have to worry about that anymore.

But Jaspora and Mother remain adamant.

BETTY: Get some milk at least.
MOTHER: (suddenly perks up) Cow's milk?
SOUTHERN LADY: Cow's milk, yes indeed. Lowfat, Nonfat, plus Goat's milk too -

MOTHER: (she makes a face) Goat? (definitively) Cow!

MOHAMMED: Regular cow's milk will be fine.

Betty gets the milk.

SOUTHERN LADY: Paper or plastic?

Jaspora has no idea.

MOHAMMED : Paper. I'm old-fashioned.

As Southern Lady adds up the bill, -

GERALD enters. COWBELL rings Tall, black, 40s, a former athlete. He strides by -- then his eyes lock on Jaspora.

SOUTHERN LADY: Hi Sweetie. Krispy Kremes -

GERALD: (eyes on JASPORA) Crisp and creamy. (she smiles back) That'll be more than delicious.

Mohammed smiles a protective territorial smile.

SOUTHERN LADY: That'll be $8.01.

Betty helps Jaspora count out her cash.

BETTY: (prompting) Thank you.

JASPORA: Thank you.

Southern Lady bags the groceries. Jaspora immediately puts the bag on her head. Southern Lady titters.

MOHAMMED: Um. Like this.

Gently, Mohammed takes the bag from Jaspora's head. Shows her the bag handles.

MOHAMMED: (cont'd) This is how we do things here.

With grace, Jaspora nods. Uses the handles.

SOUTHERN LADY: (to JASPORA) You'll be all right, Sweetie. You got horse sense.
MOTHER: Horses? Cows better.
SOUTHERN LADY: Then cow sense. Welcome to America. Y'all come back now, y'hear?

As they exit, Gerald holds the door.

GERALD: (to JASPORA) Welcome.

Gerald has an open box of donuts. Hands Jaspora one.

GERALD: (cont'd) Sweets for the sweet.

Jaspora smiles. Mother too. Each takes a donut.

JASPORA: Thank you.

Mohammed takes the door from Gerald.

MOHAMMED: No, thank you.

Betty hesitates, eyeing the donuts.

GERALD: How about you, baby?
BETTY: (tempted) Better not.

They go. Gerald watches a moment.

GERALD: WNBA in town? Chick is basketball tall.
SOUTHERN LADY: Supermodel skinny.

Gerald nods, eats. Offers Southern Lady. She eats.

GERALD: Got any idea where --?
SOUTHERN LADY: Public housing, other side of the tracks. You know where they all stay.
GERALD : What about her handlers? Church group?
SOUTHERN LADY: Out-of-towners. Carpet-bagger liberals.
GERALD: And the mom! Mind you, she was a dime-piece in her day.
SOUTHERN LADY: Get on her good side and you're half-way home. (eats) This stuff is better than sex.
GERALD : I wouldn't go that far.

Southern Lady goes fo another, Gerald closes the box, scrunches his face as an endearment and exits.

109

SOUTHERN LADY: Y'all come back, Sweetie --
(drops it) Ah fuck it.

As she polishes off the donut,

SCENE 3

Inside the apartment, -

*Mohammed with paperwork, on his cellphone. Mother in
the kitchen. Tenderizes meat -- she uses a ketchup bottle to
whack it. She swings hard.*

*Betty futzes with the broken dishwasher. It only gets worse.
In the bedroom, Jaspora disrobes. It takes time. She is very
thin. Mother crosses the room on the way to Jaspora.*

MOHAMMED: Go ahead. Speak in your own
language. You have every right.

Resumes work.

In their language, no accents, very clear:

MOTHER: (holding the ketchup bottle) You call this a
tool?
JASPORA: Maybe you need to learn how to use it.
MOTHER: Nothing works! All these toys -- buttons,
electrics, fire, fountains of running water for your
hands and for your ass -- but no real tools! What kind

of people are these? Betty with her head up the machine's ass -

JASPORA: And Muhammad?

MOTHER: On that other toy, stuck to his ear. Talking into it like an asshead. And that tone of theirs, talking to us as if we were children -

JASPORA: We are. Everything is newborn.

MOTHER: Don't believe it.

JASPORA: Be a child, Mother. Learn everything again, new, for the first time. Be a child for the first time in your life.

MOTHER: (considering) Hmmn! (noticing her semi-dress) Getting naked for him?

JASPORA: Shush. I have to wash my robes.

MOTHER: Muhammad. Almost like one of us. But not.

Jaspora puts on the hotel-style terry cloth robe.

MOTHER: (cont'd) Don't take too long. He's waiting.

JASPORA: For me?

MOTHER: Grow up, Child. Grow up fast.

Mother returns to the kitchen.

Jaspora looks at herself in the mirror.

Betty, unable to fix the dishwasher and verging on mini panic attack, ducks outdoors for a smoke. Gerald is there.

BETTY: Hey. What're you --?

GERALD: I ain't no stalker. I live here. (nods inside)
They dig the Krispy Kremes?
BETTY: Not really. They'd never eaten anything so
sweet in their lives.
GERALD: Not quite coconuts and alligator meat.
BETTY: Crocodile actually. Alligators are in Florida.
Crocks are African. (beat) You look familiar.
GERALD: I got that kind of face.
BETTY: Not the face.
GERALD: You a sports-fan?
BETTY: (as an answer) I'm from Chicago.
GERALD: Can I bum one?

Bums a cigarette off her as she studies him.

BETTY: Baseball player? Football? Boxer?
GERALD: With a face like this?
BETTY: I swear it's on the tip of my mind....
GERALD It's been awhile.
BETTY: You did something bad, didn't ya?
GERALD: You're getting warmer.
BETTY: You cheated!
GERALD: I took an over-the-counter anti-histamine,
nobody told me it was a banned substance -
BETTY: Oh snap! You're that guy! (snaps fingers)
Gerald Something. You had to give your gold medal
back, didn't you?
GERALD: Bring it all back, why don't you?
BETTY: Man, you were the fastest dude I ever saw.
Burst off that start block like some kind of springbok.

I'll never forget the way your chest muscles -- the tendons -- the way they engorged. And your ass muscles -
GERALD: Here we go.
BETTY: It was like your ass cheeks were two wild animals, two fat ferrets or meerkats going at under a blanket -
GERALD: Thanks for remembering.

Starts to go.

BETTY: Wait. I'm sorry, but it's one of those seminal moments in sports history. (beat) I was so sorry when I heard the news. I really believed you were that fast.
GERALD: I was. That wasn't trick photography.
BETTY: Yeah, but. I thought you did it without a stimulant. (ruefully) I guess there's always a stimulant. And when you had to give it back, the medal, and the things they said -

Suddenly she's crying.

GERALD: You must be buggin.
BETTY: I said I'm sorry! You're a bolt outta the blue. You kinda jumped into my imagination. I wanted to believe in you, that's all. I wanted to believe.

She cries. Finally he gives her his handkerchief.

GERALD: It really was over-the-counter.

BETTY: I knew you didn't do it on purpose!

GERALD: But the muthafucka who come in second, who's got my gold medal? He was doing the same shit! We took all kinds of shit to perform. That's what counted. The way we performed. But when the hammer came down, suddenly I was the only dude done dishonor to his flag.

BETTY: Who am I to cry?

GERALD: You're not the first. Guess I must have struck a national nerve somehow. Hey. Don't cry! I got my health, I'm still pretty and I can still run my ass off.

They laugh.

BETTY: You live here?

GERALD: Hey, it's a long way down.

BETTY: God. You used to have commercials, sneaker deals, the whole shebang.

GERALD: I'm a *hitblit*. Had it but lost it. It's cool. In the „hood, disgrace and dishonor have a certain appeal. Plus I like Hotlanta, got some jammin hotspots. It's the El Lay of the South. And the inmates run the asylum. (off her react) Us folks in charge for once.

BETTY: People of color? Theyr'e everywhere. It's weird. We just brought over two more.

GERALD: So I see. Tell me about the girl. Ethiopian?

BETTY: Somali Bantu.

GERALD: You mean like BLACK HAWK DOWN?

114

BETTY: Kinda, I guess.

GERALD: Pretty bad over there?

BETTY: Not fun. They were slaves.

GERALD: So were we.

BETTY: Hey, I'm a slave to my credit card, but we're talking stone cold semi-human rape and murder kinda slavery.

GERALD: Her too?

BETTY: (shrugs) I haven't asked.

GERALD: Christian?

BETTY: Muslim.

GERALD: Kinda inconvenient these days.

BETTY: Lotta folks trying to get them to convert.

GERALD: You?

BETTY: I don't mess with faith.

GERALD: She speak some kinda Buntu-Bantu-Swahili kinda thang? Or does she speak English?

BETTY: All things considered, her English is pretty amazing.

GERALD: Where's her man?

BETTY: Excuse me?

GERALD: Woman that fine got to have a man.

BETTY: Gerald, this ain't 20 questions. Jaspora -

GERALD: That her name?

BETTY: Guess it is a little miraculous that she's free.

GERALD: You free? (off her react) Hey. Don't hate the playa.

BETTY: Whatever, Cowboy. This tete-a-tete is just about tetted out.

Betty starts to go in. Stops as she sees --

115

Jaspora. Then Mohammed. Although they are not even looking at each other, there is something intimate about them together in the room. Betty hesitates.

GERALD: Come on, Girl. This is the South. You gots to relax down here! Let's go downtown to Vickery's on Crescent Ave.
BETTY: You're asking the wrong girl.
GERALD: Love the one you're with, baby.
BETTY: It's Betty.
GERALD: Like I said.

She closes the door. Remains outside.

BETTY: Can I smoke?
GERALD: You can do whatever you want.

As they exit, -

SCENE 4

Inside the apartment.

Mother cooks a stew. She keeps finding items whose purpose eludes her. But instead offsetting them aside, she uses them to her advantage (whether they were meant for such use or not). Her cooking is an adventure. Is a certain substance flour or Ajax? As she chucks one or the other into the stew, --

Jaspora washes her traditional robe in the sink.

Mohammed hangs up the phone and puts away the paperwork. He speaks in ARABIC.

MOHAMMED: *Kaifa haloki?*
JASPORA: English.

He speaks in SWAHILI.

MOHAMMED: *Habari zako.*
JASPORA: No. English!

He speaks in BANTU.

JASPORA: (cont'd) Muhammad!!
MOHAMMED: You sure?
JASPORA: I need to learn!
MOHAMMED : You need to learn to use the washer/dryer. It's a lot better. I have quarters! (off her laughter) It's just the way we do things here.

Mohammed places several stacks of quarters on a counter.

JASPORA: Next time.

Jaspora continues washing.

JASPORA: (cont'd) Arabic, Swahili, Bantu -
MOHAMMED: Just showing off.
JASPORA: You have many tongues?

MOHAMMED: Languages? I lost count. Not that hard, really. All you have to do is listen. You just have to want to. (beat) How many tongues to you have?
JASPORA: Just one tongue. But it is talented.
MOHAMMED: (coughs) How did your English get so good?
JASPORA: The Voice of America!
MOHAMMED: The radio?
JASPORA: I listened every day. (quotes with pride) We the People In order to form a more perfect union Establish justice and ensure domestic tranquility -
MOHAMMED: Wow!
JASPORA: Sounds good?
MOHAMMED On your tongue? Yes. Better than I remembered.

As she washes by hand, -
Mohammed pulls out a small RADIO.

MOHAMMED: (cont'd) For your mother. Atlanta has good radio.

Fiddles with the dial. COMMODORES "I'M EASY" plays.

MOHAMMED: (cont'd) Not quite the Voice of America, but -
JASPORA: Very good!
MOHAMMED: There's an arabic station here somewhere, -

Finds traditional ARABIC SINGING of the Quran.

Mother reacts.

Jaspora changes the dial.

JASPORA: American. We are American.

Jaspora finds a Celine Dion song.

She breathes it in.

Mohammed nods, understanding.

MOHAMMED: Have you heard of Sidney Poitier?
(she shakes her head no) You will. He got rid of his
island accent by listening to the radio. He became a
big star.
JASPORA: Like Celine Dion?
MOHAMMED: Sure. I guess. She still has her accent.
(fiddles with the radio) Whatever you want. So many
new things. And yes, you are American. (beat) And
it's really too kind to make us dinner, there's certainly
no need -
JASPORA: Mother makes good stew.
MOHAMMED: Perhaps I should call Betty in, --?
JASPORA: Let her smoke! We make her nervous. (off
his react) Sit.
MOHAMMED: Refugee Services says that you need
to repeat basic lessons. "Don't touch the hot stove.

Don't touch the hot stove!" And here you are fixing me a meal!

JASPORA: Don't touch the hot stove? You only need to say it once!

MOHAMMED: All you need to do is touch.

JASPORA: Thank you for the robe.

MOHAMMED: It's from the Four Corners Hotel. They provide robes with every room. We've worked out a deal to obtain jobs for you *Mushunguli*. Now when you're cleaning their rooms you can feel equal to the guests.

JASPORA: I'm not equal?

MOHAMMED: You are.

Jaspora holds up her hand-cleaned robes to the light. Tiny FLASH of rainbow colors through a prism. A perfect moment until -

Mother grunts.

JASPORA: Dinner is ready.

Mother suddenly cries out, curses.

JASPORA: (cont'd) Don't touch the stove!

Jaspora laughs. Mother flashes her an evil look.

MOHAMMED: Only need to say it once. (turns away to hide smile) I'll get Betty.

Mohammed goes to the door. Betty is not there. When he turns back, Jaspora beckons.

MOTHER: Muhammad.
MOHAMMED: Mohammed, yes.
MOTHER: Muslim?
MOHAMMED: Partly.
JASPORA: Which part?

Mother harrumphs. Returns to the stove.

MOHAMMED: She can tell. I'm not a man of God.
JASPORA: (RE: MOTHER) She is Muslim.
MOHAMMED: And you?
JASPORA: I want to believe in many things. But I need to see them first.
MOHAMMED: I feel the same way. (beat) You'll see that life is life, very similar. It's just the little things that get confusing. People think you *Mushunguli* will have trouble, living so long without technology. But I think you'll do fine in this country. Underneath the laptops and IPODs, people are just people. (beat) It's amazing that you've come South. Your people's history as a slave class -- many of the folk you'll meet were once just like you.
JASPORA: Were you like us, Muhammad?
MOHAMMED: (coughs) In what way?
JASPORA: Were you a slave once too? (off MOHAMMED's react) It is not so bad to be a slave. But it is better to be free.

MOHAMMED: It's better to be free.

Mother serves stew. Jaspora takes them to the table.

JASPORA: Now I am Bantu -slash -- American. I can
do anything. I can sing. Like Celine Dion.
MOHAMMED: You can.
JASPORA: Was it that way for you, Muhammad?
MOHAMMED: What?
JASPORA: When you became free?
MOHAMMED: (sputters) Free? But – I'm -(stops
himself)
JASPORA: But what?

*Mohammed rises, very much out of sorts but trying to
cover it.*

MOHAMMED: I should go.
JASPORA: Muhammad -
MOHAMMED: Save your food. Use the refrigerator.
There's Rubbermaid in the cabinet. Sleep well.
Tomorrow we get you a job at the Four Corners. I'll
be here in the morning. (to MOTHER) Goodnight
Mother.

*Mohammed ducks out. Stands on the landing alone. As
soon as he's out, he wants to come in again.*

MOHAMMED: (cont'd) I'm not free.

Very alone, he exits.

Jaspora fingers her robe.

MOTHER: (grunts)

Mother gives her stew. Jaspora about to eat, notices the Ajax next to the flour.

As she chews fatalistically, -

Mother turns on TV. BLUE LIGHT reflects off her face. Cast sings:

CAST: I HAVE HEARD THE WISEST OF WISDOM AND I HAVE DINED IN PALACES AND KINGDOMS BUT NOTHING IS AS BEAUTIFUL AS WHEN SHE BELIEVES....

SCENE 5

VICKERY's -- an Atlanta eatery.

Betty is on her third apple martini. Gerald eats ribs -- greasy fingers.

BETTY: You know what they say.
GERALD: They say a lotta things.
BETTY: They say martinis are like breasts. One's not enough and three's too many! (knocks hers back) Uh-oh! I'm in trouble now.

GERALD: Maybe you oughta eat something. Have some garlic bread, sop up that mess.

BETTY: Tryna give me garlic breath? I may wanna kiss somebody.

GERALD: Have a rib.

BETTY: Tryna give me greasy fingers?

GERALD: I'm tryna cool you out.

BETTY: I'm just gonna have one more. Then it'll be like sleeping with two women!

GERALD: Huh?

BETTY: Four breasts!

GERALD: Whatever. Drink this, why dontcha. (pushes her the water glass)

BETTY: Damn! You sucked those ribs clean.

GERALD: Damn straight. I could eat a bucket of these. But they cost as much as my damn shoes.

BETTY: (a little too loud) That's what's wrong with this country! FREE RIBS! *AMANDLA*!! FREE RIBS OR DIE!

GERALD: Keep it down baby.

BETTY: Just exercising my free speech.

GERALD: Down South free speech will get you kilt.

BETTY: What is this, some kind of parallel universe?

GERALD: Absolutely. I had to shave off my beard after 9-11. Look like Osama, that's a bad idea. The South takes Homeland Security serious as a heart attack.

BETTY: Why didn't they keep our homeland secure from home foreclosures? Terrorists -- what about subprime mortgage lenders? Those are the real terrorists! Not to mention the Christian terrorists -

GERALD: Don't mention 'em. This is Bush Country. The ribs are overpriced and the walls have ears. In this room, right now, there's somebody listening, just waiting for you to try your progressive Chicago shit on for size. Make one mistake, they'll send you to County Jail, you'll get lost in the system. Do ya in the old style, won't even be able to find your name.

BETTY: Mohammed Chang! He'd find me!

GERALD: Say what?

BETTY: My partner in crime! He's got superpowers!

GERALD: Mohammed Chang? What kinda fool name is that?

BETTY: Chang. Most common name in the world.

GERALD: I thought Jones was. Or Smith.

BETTY: Chang kicks Jones's ass. Chang takes Smith's lunch money.

GERALD: Mohammed? Black Muslim? That's cool.

Betty does a little martial arts hand chop mixed with an Ali shuffle.

BETTY: Muhammad Ali meets Jackie Chan! Hero to the tired, the weak, the huddled masses. And mighty good at his job.

GERALD: Which is?

BETTY: Resettling the slaves of the world.

GERALD: Slaves? He should start right here. Drive fifty miles, might as well be in the middle of GONE WITH THE WIND. Hell, right here in Atlanta. (beat) When all my shit went down, I couldn't get a table at my favorite restaurant, and soon I couldn't afford to eat there anyway. My lady left me, took the kids. No one looked me in the eye. Then I saw. I was the Black Christ on the Cross or some shit. Folks looked at me and saw their own guilty shit reflected back. They saw worse things than I ever dreamed of doing. But that was them. That's how I got free. Now I just let it be. The South don't fool me. And it sure as hell won't clown me neither.

BETTY: Buy me a drink.

GERALD: I don't think so.

BETTY: Fine! I'll buy it myself.

GERALD: I'll buy, but give me five minutes before you get completely shitfaced.

BETTY: I'm fine.

GERALD: I got a business proposition.

BETTY: You proposing?

GERALD: I said business.

BETTY: With me?

GERALD: Through you. Jaspora. (beat) I think I can make her some money.

BETTY: Man, don't even try to pimp.

GERALD: (flares up) Pimp? See? That's beyond ignorant.

BETTY: You're shooting for her panties!

GERALD: I guess your five minutes were up about an hour ago.

BETTY: Why aren't you shooting for mine?

He gets up.

BETTY: (cont'd) Where you going?

126

GERALD: To pay up. Cause this night is over. Strange as may seem, I actually think about other things than sex.
BETTY: What if I don't?

She touches his leg.

GERALD: Turn on ESPN CLASSICS. Masturbate to my wild animal ass. That's as close are you'll get to my butt.
BETTY: Whatever!
GERALD: Don't get ganky on me!
BETTY: Ganky? I am not ganky. I'm from Chicago. We are not ganky in Chicago. We are sportsfans. We drink and smoke all night, and talk about having sex with everyone from Tiger to MJ to Venus and Serena. Get over it. Grow a sense of humor, Gerald.
GERALD: I'm sensitive about certain words.
BETTY: Well I am drunk!
GERALD: I'm trying to talk business.
BETTY: Don't talk. Do. Do do do.

They stare at each other.

GERALD: Okay. Straight up no chaser. Just one look at that Ebony Princess and it all come to me. This is the plan -
BETTY: Hold on. (to an UNSEEN WAITER) *Una mas!* (sober, to GERALD) Okay. You got five minutes.

As he begins to speak, -

SCENE 6

The next morning.

Mother at the TV. She eats stew. Theme from Teletubbies.

MOTHER: Time for Teletubbies.

Jaspora appears in nondescript Western-style workclothes. They cling to her long lean body -- her ankles and wrists protrude. Over her head she still wears an African scarf.

Mother sees her, harrumphs.

A haggard Betty smokes on the landing. Eyes behind dark glasses. Knocks.

Jaspora opens the door.

JASPORA: Muhammad -
BETTY: Mohammed can't be here. (off her react) Had to drive to Charlotte. Getting a client out of a legal jam. I'll take you to the meeting. (off JASPORA"s look, angry) Hey! I work for you too!
JASPORA: Are you ill?
BETTY: I'm fine. Believe me, it's nothing I don't deserve. Woulda been all right, but I forgot to eat. How many martinis did I drink last night? I lost count.
JASPORA: Martini?

BETTY: One day I'll teach you about 'em.

Jaspora goes inside. Betty checks her watch.

BETTY: (cont'd) We really oughta get going. Traffic --

Jaspora fills a bowl of stew.

JASPORA: Eat.
BETTY: I couldn't. No I really couldn't.
JASPORA: Eat.

Stalemate. Betty succumbs.

BETTY: Not quite Rice Krispies.

Jaspora leads Betty inside.

MOTHER: Time for Teletubbies! (waves)
BETTY: (watches along with her) The Beatles for 3-year-olds.
JASPORA: (using her fingers as a creepy-crawly thing) Beetles?
BETTY: Let me have a look at you.

Betty looks over Jaspora's new get-up. Jaspora models it unhappily.

JASPORA: I don't like it.

BETTY: Better to fit in, wear your Dickies. Jobs are hard to come by these days. How tall are you? (JASPORA shrugs) Tall enough.

Betty looks her over, up and down.

BETTY: (cont'd) You ever read style mags? I'll buy you one. Style's self-explanatory. You'll have more fun with it than a flush toilet. Probably where you'll read it too.
JASPORA: You have good style.
BETTY: Not me, and especially not today.

Mother reacts to the TV.

BETTY: (cont'd) (RE: MOTHER) She okay?
JASPORA: She's learning English.
BETTY: Of a fashion. (to MOTHER) Thanks for the stew.

Jaspora and Mother whisper something.

JASPORA: She wants cow's milk.
BETTY: We'll pick up a carton on the way.
MOTHER: Teletubbies come out to play!

They leave. Mother smiles wide at the TV.

CAST: WHEN SHE BELIEVES WHEN SHE BEILEVES....

SCENE 7

As Mother continues to watch -

Betty and Jaspora enter an office. GLENNA enters on the run. Business suit and Dunkin Donuts coffee to go.

GLENNA: (to BETTY mostly) Sorry I'm late! Traffic. You'd think we were in Los Angeles! All these latte-drinking Northerners in their SUVs gumming up the highways. Are you from Georgia?
BETTY: I'm one of those SUV Northerners. Betty Dubuisson, Refugee Resettlement. I think you know my associate Mister Chang.

No reaction from Glenna. Betty presents Jaspora's paperwork.

BETTY: (cont'd) (gesturing) This is Jaspora.
GLENNA: Jaspora? My what a different name.
BETTY: She arrived last week from a refugee camp in Kenya. Idea is to get her a job.
GLENNA: "When you wish upon a star...."
BETTY: More than a wish.
GLENNA: If not, there's always welfare.
BETTY: Let's hope not.

Jaspora seems very subdued. Glenna looks through paperwork.

GLENNA: Literacy?

BETTY: She speaks beautifully. We're shooting for GED, high school equivalency, -

GLENNA: Meaning she's way below median range.

BETTY: She's excellent for someone who survived a civil war.

GLENNA: Well we haven't had one of those in quite a long time, have we? (beat) Skills?

BETTY: Custodial, cleaning, laundry -

GLENNA: History of illness?

JASPORA: No illness.

GLENNA: (to BETTY) We've been burned recently. Some of our recent West African hires have turned out to have significant HIV.

JASPORA: No HIV.

GLENNA: (to BETTY) Unfortunately we know a lot more about disease since we started these programs. Schistosomiasis, roundworms, tapeworms, all kinds of parasitic diseases. That doesn't go down so very well in a hotel situation, or for that matter in any kind of hospitality job.

JASPORA: No HIV!

BETTY: We told you; she's clean.

GLENNA: We're a progressive institution, but things have changed. Orange alerts, threats, it's created a climate of fear. Beyond which, the economy has been unkind to say the least. We're laying off trusted employees as it is.

BETTY: Wait a second, I don't know if I'm understanding you correctly.

GLENNA: We're not going to be able to take anymore Bantu or Somali or -

BETTY: Or what? Muslims? Black people? I thought we had an agreement, -

GLENNA: Look, I don't want to offend anyone -

BETTY: Why stop now?

GLENNA: May we speak alone?

BETTY: Now you're sensitive to her feelings?

GLENNA: I'm sorry you don't like what you're hearing. But the world has changed. Whether you like it or not. (RE: JASPORA) Please?

BETTY: She stays.

GLENNA: Very well then. The Bantu are virtually a Stone Age tribe.

BETTY: Stone Age? Like Fred Flintstone?

GLENNA: Like no experience in the civilized world. Like totally incompatible with big city life. They've been subjugated! They're too used to violence -- This isn't personal, it's based on first-hand observation -

BETTY: I can see you've been studying.

GLENNA: Have you ever given them IQ tests?

BETTY: Those have been largely discredited -

GLENNA: Not by us. Every employee takes a specially designed exam. The average for a white American is about 100. For an American black about 86. For an African refugee – we're talking 60.

BETTY: That's how you rate a person?

GLENNA: That's how we tell a mental vegetable.

BETTY: Very sensitive choice of words.

GLENNA: I asked you if we could talk alone.

BETTY: I'd like to see what test score you'd get in the Somali desert.

GLENNA: That's a test I'll never have to take. (stands) And now, if you'll excuse me -

BETTY: No, I don't think I will.

Betty and Jaspora rise. As they leave, -

GLENNA: Feel superior if it helps you. But let me pass along a personal observation - (beat) You're too close.

BETTY: Am I?

GLENNA: You can't see. It's not your fault.

BETTY: Don't you feel the least bit guilty?

GLENNA: Why? I didn't do anything.

Glenna leaves before Betty can respond.

JASPORA: No job?

BETTY: This job sucks anyway.

Immediate light change.

SCENE 8

OUTDOORS, -

The cement landing. Betty walks to Mohammed, in media res.

MOHAMMED: WHAT?

BETTY: She was such a bitch! She said this all in front of Jaspora!

MOHAMMED: Why didn't you send Jaspora out of the room?

BETTY: I don't think she understood -

MOHAMMED: Her English is excellent.

BETTY: She didn't say anything.

MOHAMMED: What is she supposed to say? What kind of vocabulary have we taught to her to express that kind of shame? (off her silence) I'll call the Hotel Workers Union, we'll get to the bottom of this.

BETTY: Leave it alone.

MOHAMMED: I CAN'T!!!

BETTY: You know your problem? You're too close.

MOHAMMED: I didn't know I had a problem.

As he takes out his cellphone, -

INDOORS, --

Jaspora goes to the bathroom.

Mother at the stove, calls out.

MOTHER: Cow's milk? (no response) No cow? Hmmph.

Jaspora plays with the toilet flush.

Mother returns to the TV. SOUNDS OF Bloomberg News stock market reports. Mother watches them with relish. Whether she understands a bit of it is another question.

OUTDOORS, -

Mohammed on the phone. Betty smokes.

MOHAMMED: I'm on hold!

BETTY: How was Charlotte?

MOHAMMED: My Zapoteca client? Hauled in as an illegal. Except he's not. I had the paperwork, but they wouldn't listen to me. They didn't know he was Zapoteca. They thought he was Afghani. They couldn't understand when he spoke nahuatl, they thought it was Arabic. They were about to call in National Security! Xenophobia is catching.

BETTY: Zapotecs look a lot like Afghanis.

MOHAMMED: They do, actually.

BETTY: Why'd you have to go to Charlotte anyway? Don't they resettlement people there?

MOHAMMED: They closed the Charlotte office. I'm wondering if we're next.

BETTY: If we close down, what are these new immigrants supposed to do? Pull themselves up by their bootstraps? They don't even have boots! (RE: JASPORA and MOTHER) So what are we gonna do with these two?

MOHAMMED: Get them on Cash Assistance, Rental Assistance. Pound the pavement. Hope Obama sees their plight among the million other fuck-ups of the last eight years. In other words, don't hold your breath.

BETTY: I know it sounds crazy, but.... I met this guy....

MOHAMMED: After how many martinis?

BETTY: (choosing to ignore) He's hiring. A local, small-business type opportunity. Black-owned.

MOHAMMED: What field?

BETTY: Fashion industry.

Mohammed hangs up.

MOHAMMED: Possibilities. You seen his portfolio?

BETTY: I believe in him. (beat) I really mishandled the meeting this morning. This will make it up to her.

MOHAMMED: Set up a meeting.

Mohammed starts to go. Betty lingers.

BETTY: Why is Jaspora single?

MOHAMMED: Why?

BETTY: Where's the husband? Where's the kids? I mean, she's not too hard to look at.

MOHAMMED: Her child died. It's in the file.

BETTY: Just one? These Bantu are baby-makers. How'd she show such restraint? Where is the husband? You gotta admit, it's awfully convenient -

MOHAMMED: There's nothing convenient about her situation.

BETTY: But on the real -

MOHAMMED: Maybe she didn't meet the right guy. (staredown) Make the meeting. There's a lot of people watching our little high wire act. If we don't step right she falls.

Mohammed exits fast.

BETTY: The right guy, huh?

She lights another cigarette.

INSIDE, -

Mother gets up, goes to the bathroom.

Jaspora lets her in. They switch places.

Mother plays with the toilet flush.

Jaspora stands, lost in the middle of the room.

TV blares Wall Street Reports, Fox News, ESPN, MTV, CNN, Tampax ads.

Jaspora experiences a panic attack. Loss of breath, lightheadedness, tears from down deep.

Finally she SCREAMS. Grabs the channel changer, haphazardly hits buttons.

Theme for MISTER ROGERS. As she weeps, the voice of Fred Rogers grows in volume. Relaxes her. Soon she is breathing normally. Still crying, she begins to hum to -

JASPORA: MISTER ROGERS WON'T YOU PLEASE PLEASE WON"T YOU PLEASE PLEASE WON'T YOU BE MY NEIGHBOR

Mother flushes the toilet.

END ACT ONE

ACT TWO

SCENE 1

Theme from TELETUBBIES in darkness. Light peaks in. Mother at the sofa, still.

MOTHER: Time for Tubby Tustard!

As she sits, -Three slightly Africanized TELETUBBIES appear -- DIPSY, PO and LALA -- dancing to the also slightly Africanized Teletubby music.

Mother dances with them. Purse in hand, she resembles a Tinky Winky in kinte cloth. She dances with an unexpected abandon. The Teletubbies support her every move. They too begin to really get down -- the Teletubbies have soul!

SOUNDS from the bedroom. Mother stops dancing.

MOTHER: (cont'd) (with irony) Time for Tubby Tustard.

The Teletubbies wave goodbye as they DISAPPEAR. Gerald appears in his briefs.

GERALD: Got any milk?
MOTHER: Cow's milk?
GERALD: Rather have a cow, huh? I always liked cows with their big eyelashes. But I don't dig cowturd. So I'll take my milk homogenized.

Opens the refrigerator, takes a pull from the carton.

GERALD: (cont'd) Got any crackers? Maybe some cookies? Nah? Back in my pro days, my trainers woulda killed me for what I ate on the sly. Only time I could feed my cookie jones was in the morning. Oh I ate me some Twinkies! Some Ho-Hos! Workout was that much sweeter. Course I never seemed to lose any weight!

Finds the stew in some tupperware.

GERALD: (cont'd) Can I eat this, Mother? (off her GRUNT) Is it hot? I like that island hot, oh I had me some times island hopping -- treat you just like royalty when you're the fastest man on the planet!

Eats. It's hotter than he can take. Gulps milk.

MOTHER: (grunts amusedly)
GERALD: Whoo, this is hella-hot! No wonder y'all stay so thin! (sucks down milk till it's empty) Remind me to buy you a cow! (beat) You speak English, honey?
MOTHER: No.
GERALD: But you understand! I can tell. I see it in your eyes. You're a sly one! Boy, the things you musta seen in your day. And I bet you used to shake your tail-feathers! I bet you still do!

MUTED cellphone rings with a message. He goes to it.

GERALD: (cont'd) Excuse me, huh?

Gerald opens his cellphone.

GERALD: (cont'd) Oh shit.

Gerald hangs up, immediately gets up and goes to the bedroom. Jaspora under the covers. Mother watches him.

GERALD: (cont'd) Gotta go, but I'll be back. We got business. This is our shot, baby. (gesturing at the bed) Keep this whole thang on the QT. You know the drill. (a kiss) Believe me when I tell you. It's gonna be beautiful.

Puts on his clothes fast. Sees Mother.

GERALD: (cont'd) You too. Be cool now. (winks, no response) By the way, you got yourself a mighty nice daughter there. Favors her momma!

He is about to leave.

Mother fixes him with her eyes.

Suddenly he understands.

GERALD: (cont'd) Right.

Fishes for his wallet. Drops several 20s on the counter.

GERALD: (cont'd) Call it a down-payment on the cow.

Winks again. This time she waves Teletubbie-style.

MOTHER: Bye-bye.

Gerald splits.

Mother gets up, inspects the cash, puts it in her purse.

Jaspora enters. Slightly zonked. Says nothing. Goes to Gerald's half-eaten stew and picks at it. Turns the RADIO on. One COMMERCIAL after another. Mother takes over. Finds the ARABIC STATION. Songs from the Quran.

For a moment, Mother prays.

Jaspora snickers at her.

They speak to each other in THEIR LANGUAGE.

MOTHER: (cont'd) Back to that, are we?
JASPORA: Relax.
MOTHER: Tramp!
JASPORA: It was good enough for you.
MOTHER: I had to.
JASPORA: So did I!
MOTHER: You don't HAVE TO do anything here.
You can sit and watch this thing all day and night -
JASPORA: YOU can sit. I have to work.
MOTHER: Work is nothing. I can work.
JASPORA: If I can't get a job, how can you?
MOTHER: If all else fails, -

She starts to move, a variation on the Teletubbies dance,
but this time seductive. Jaspora laughs despite herself.

JASPORA: You're too old!
MOTHER: Not too old for that! Americans are so old!
Old and fat and ugly. I'm too good for them!
JASPORA: You're a real princess.

Mother shows an amazing sense of humor and sexuality in
her moves. Jaspora isn't surprised, she's seen it before.

MOTHER: So. How was he?
JASPORA: Shush.

MOTHER: Hussy, I heard you squeal. And his color. He's so light, like baby shit! Is his ass that light too?

JASPORA: Pink. But very, very strong. He has a lot of muscles. A lot of ass muscles!

MOTHER: Men are strange here!

JASPORA: What do you know about men here?

MOTHER: Like our Muhammad. So timid. The other night, if he played it right, he could have had both of us!

JASPORA: Don't make fun of him. He's our hope.

MOTHER: Who's making fun. I'm telling the truth. Wonder what color his ass is?

JASPORA: You'll never know!

MOTHER: Will you? (beat) What? You like Muhammad? Don't be stupid.

JASPORA: Shut up.

MOTHER: You'll get fat and old one day. Your tits will touch your belly. But you won't be stupid the way you were when you were beautiful. (beat) Tell me to shut up! Mind yourself.

JASPORA: I know what I'm doing.

MOTHER: Child! Back in camp you'd cry when they played their stupid star-spangled banner. Voice of America? Soft in the head! You'll believe anything!

JASPORA: Not anything. (beat) There's business tonight. You're nowhere in this country unless you do business, and do it well.

MOTHER: I know business. This Gerald will try to use you. He can't do it alone, but he thinks he can. It's just like home. Try to look pretty. Let the men think

they're making the decisions. And stay very very alert. (turns off RADIO) Gerald promised me a cow.
JASPORA: Where would you put it? (beat) We'll get something better.
MOTHER: What's better than a cow? Nothing in this country is better than a cow!!

Jaspora nearly puts the terry cloth robe on. Stops.

JASPORA: "When you wish upon a star...."

As she stares at it, -

Mother again attempts to pray.

CAST: NOW, ALL OF LIFE IS JUST PASSING TIME UNTIL ONCE AGAIN YOUR EYES LOOK INTO MINE NOW I HAVE BEEN ADORED BY A STRANGER AND I HAVE HEARD THE WHISPERING ANGEL....

SCENE 2

Mohammed outside the mini-mart. Goes to the Homies dispenser. A bit surreptitious. Puts quarters in, about to turn the crank when -

SOUTHERN LADY: Hey Sweetie.
MOHAMMED: Hey.

Blushing a bit, he turns the crank. Pulls out a Homie.

SOUTHERN LADY: I thought that stuff was for kids.
MOHAMMED: It's for my nephew.
SOUTHERN LADY: Sure, that's what they all say.
(beat) Who'dya get? (MOHAMMED shows her)
Whew! Is that little fella in a wheelchair?
MOHAMMED: Yeah.
SOUTHERN LADY: I thought these Homies was little
gangbangers. I didn't know they was cripples too. (as
she investigates) You think he got shot? Drive-by?
MOHAMMED: I don't know.
SOUTHERN LADY: I didn't ask what you know, I
asked what you thought.
MOHAMMED: I think he's a mystery, and I like that.

He puts in more quarters.

SOUTHERN LADY: How many little guys you got?
MOHAMMED: Just about the whole collection.
SOUTHERN LADY: That's a lotta quarters.
MOHAMMED: They're my vice.
SOUTHERN LADY: Mine are sweet things. Sweet tea
and Krispy Kremes, chocolate chip, and a little sweet
potato pie with whipped cream on top. Keep you
warm at night.

*He buys another Homie. By his reaction, we know it's a
good one.*

SOUTHERN LADY: (cont'd) Who'dya get this time?
MOHAMMED: One I've coveted.

SOUTHERN LADY: Coveted? (investigating) Oooh. She's pretty. But how come she's wearing dark glasses and that long coat? What's she got to hide?
MOHAMMED: Therein lies the mystery.

Betty appears.

SOUTHERN LADY: Hey Sweetie.
BETTY: Hay is for horses!

Slightly awkward pause as all three stand there.
Mohammed tries to smile the Lady back inside her store.

SOUTHERN LADY: (to MOHAMMED) Oh. I'll let you play with your toys.
MOHAMMED: I don't play with them, -

Southern Lady exits inside her store.

BETTY: Busted, huh?
MOHAMMED: People don't understand.
BETTY: I understand. You like what you like.

Mohammed pockets his Homies.

MOHAMMED: Let's go.
BETTY: I scheduled the meeting at the apartment.
MOHAMMED: Why?
BETTY: Seemed easiest.
MOHAMMED: Doesn't your friend have an office?

BETTY: Just seemed easier.

MOHAMMED: Anything else I need to know?

BETTY: I know you're mad at me. You don't think I'm serious about what we're doing. Well I am. Serious as a home foreclosure.

MOHAMMED: That's serious.

BETTY: Did you change their minds at the hotel?

MOHAMMED: (shakes head no) We had a conference call yesterday -- caseworkers in Roanoke, Boise, San Diego --same story. No jobs, everything drying up. This is not the picture of this country we sold the refugees. Not by a long-shot.

BETTY: Alternatives?

MOHAMMED : Christian groups poised to pick up the slack. They offer jobs, even housing. But that doesn't help our Muslim friends, unless they convert.

BETTY: Are you gonna ask them?

MOHAMMED: My life is devoted to man's relation to man. Not man's relation to God.

BETTY: Heavy.

MOHAMMED: Look, uh. Betty, if I raised my voice the other * day, --

BETTY: Where's your life? Really?

MOHAMMED: I didn't hear you right.

BETTY: Family? Friends? Where?

MOHAMMED: Here. Always here.

BETTY: Atlanta?

MOHAMMED Well I'm here now.

BETTY: Anywhere you lay your head is home? That's sad.

MOHAMMED: Is it?

BETTY: Well, what team do you root for? I mean, what's the home team? Cause we all got a home team. Who's your team?

MOHAMMED: I don't really follow team sports.

BETTY: Where you're from says so much about who you are! How you vote! If you call it soda or pop!

MOHAMMED: I don't care for soft drinks.

BETTY: Like I'm from Chicago. That says everything about me!

MOHAMMED: Does it?

BETTY: (slightly confused) Yeah, I think it does.

MOHAMMED: When I see you I don't see The Loop or The Chicago Red Sox -

BETTY: White Sox.

MOHAMMED: I see you.

BETTY: Geez. That's sad.

MOHAMMED: Why sad?

BETTY: That's all you see?

MOHAMMED: It's a whole world.

BETTY: Is it?

Mohammed goes. Betty follows.

SCENE 3

Jaspora and Gerald sit on the bed. He has the paper.

GERALD: New York Times.

JASPORA: New York?

GERALD: You'll get there, baby.

JASPORA: Is it a city or a state?

GERALD: It's a state of mind.

JASPORA: Is it hot?

GERALD: Very hot and very cold.

JASPORA: It's confusing.

GERALD: It is.

JASPORA: New York is North?

GERALD : Yep.

JASPORA: Atlanta is South.

GERALD: The very heart.

JASPORA: Are there slaves in New York?

GERALD: Oh yeah.

JASPORA: North and South are the same.

GERALD: Here's the thing. Down South, a man my color can get as close as he want, long as he don't get too big. Up North, he can get as big as he want, long as he don't get too close. That's an old joke from back in the day. It's different now. But it's still the same. Down deep, on the real.

JASPORA: I like it on the real.

GERALD: So who you like to groove to? Who wets your whiskers? Who puts the rock in your sock? T-Pain? Li'l Wayne?

JASPORA: Celine Dion.

GERALD: Celine Di--? No. Uh-uh. No can do.

JASPORA: Why?

GERALD: This is Atlanta! The Dirty South! You gotta represent.

JASPORA: Rep-re-sent?

GERALD: Who you are. What you listen to. What you wear. You gotta choose, baby.

JASPORA: Choose? You just are.

GERALD: You got a chance to re-make yourself, foot to head. I'll admit, it's a lotta work. But you can leave your past behind. This I know. (beat) I'm sure Celine Dion is a nice person, but you are in charge -- you can burn your own CDs! You don't gotta listen to somebody else's mess no mo'. That's in the Constitution somewheres.

JASPORA: It's not.

GERALD: Well it oughta be. (winks) I'll bring you some tunes. Southern hard-core, chopped and screwed, slowed and throwed. We'll get ya started right quick.

Knock-knock; then again a little more persistent. Mother opens the door.

OUTDOORS, -

IDA LOU stands smiling on the landing.

IDA LOU: Well hello! (extends a hand) Welcome to Atlanta! I'm Ida Lou.

Mother takes her hand. Says nothing.

IDA LOU: (cont'd) You must be -- now don't tell me -- Mother Abdekadir! We're just so pleased to have you and your daughter Jaspora in Decatur right here alongside us.

She waits to be invited in. Mother makes no move.

IDA LOU: (cont'd) I'm a native. My family's lived in Atlanta since I was a gleam in my father's eye! Same old house with the same white picket fence. (beat) But this apartment complex is very comfy. There's a lovely Rwandan couple around the corner! You two should visit, I'm sure you have a lot in common!

Mother enjoys not having the language or culture to respond.

IDA LOU (cont'd) Perhaps we should go -- inside --? (no react) It's just that it's a little warm out here. (beat) Of course, it does get awfully cold down here too, we even had a snow last spring. Snow's liable to befuddle you -- some of our African brethren described it as "from heaven." In this country you need a friend, someone to invite you in for hot chocolate by a warm fire. Not today, of course -- today, you'll wish for a tall cold glass of sweet tea -- wouldn't that be nice? But one day you'll be awfully glad to have a friend. Which is why I'm here.

She presents Mother with several flyers.

IDA LOU: (cont'd) We're having a cook-out at the Ted before the Braves game next Thursday. You should come! You'll love baseball. We're a real community, a real family. We meet three times a week. Not just Sunday. Bible class on Tuesdays.

Rummage sales, quilt-making, even workshops in investment opportunities. Unlike some of other tabernacles, we've made sure to grow with the times. We like to live our own lives, IN HIS PRESENCE. (beat) That's the name of our church. Join us!
MOTHER: Not Christ. (shakes a single finger) Muslim.
IDA LOU: We know. (beat) Life is change. This is a good one for you, believe me. We don't mean to push, but we're so excited to offer you this opportunity as we fight the good fight against the forces of evil that have so much hatred in their hearts for our freedoms -
MOTHER: 9/11? Not me.
IDA LOU: Of course not you! We know all Muslims aren't terrorists! But there's people who won't see the difference. That's why you'll want to choose your friends, your family, -
MOTHER: Family?
IDA LOU: This is a new time, a new country, a New South. It's God's country.
MOTHER: God is great.
IDA LOU: He is, isn't He.

For a moment, both women smile in agreement. Teletubbie theme.

Mother starts to close the door. Ida Lou gets her foot in the door.

IDA LOU: (cont'd) When the government turns its back -- and it will -- when the job goes South -- so to

153

speak -- when your Allah promises you a better life in the next but can do nothing about the one you got now -- Remember we're IN HIS PRESENCE. Folks like you have been getting spiritual balm from folks like us for well on three hundred years. We can't be all wrong, now can we?? (her best smile) You keep those flyers.

MOTHER: Time for tubby bye-bye.

Mother closes the door. Ida Lou stands warrior-like.

IDA LOU: You're in his presence whether you like it or not.

Her smile fades. She leaves.

A moment later, more knock-knocks.

Grumbling, Mother opens the door.

Mohammed and Betty stand outside on the landing.

MOHAMMED: Hello, Mother.

They enter. From inside, Jaspora appears alongside Gerald. She once again wears her traditional robes, although they seem by far less colorful. He wears flashy, tailored clothes.

MOHAMMED: (cont'd) You.

GERALD : Gerald Bang-bang McClellan, that's my name don't wear it out.

They shake hands.

MOHAMMED: Mohammed Chang.
GERALD: (little martial arts/Ali shuffle) Muhammad Ali meets Jackie Chan. (winks at BETTY) Hey.
BETTY: (irritated) Let's get started, shall we?
MOHAMMED: Bang-bang?
GERALD: From the bang of the gun to the bang of the tape I never stopped and I never will. I ran just like the Devil was on my ass trying to punk me. And he chased my butt all the way to Olympic gold.
MOHAMMED: I don't follow track and field.

Jaspora is very quiet.

MOHAMMED: (cont'd) Are you all right?
JASPORA: Yes, Muhammad.
MOHAMMED: Are you sure? You seem -
JASPORA: I am fine, Muhammad.
BETTY: Maybe we oughta get down to biz-
MOHAMMED: This is business.

Gerald takes over. He has a semi-gospel-preacher rhetorical style.

GERALD: Them lemme lay it on the line. It's been a trial trying to find my way ever since I gave up running. Us athletes don't got pensions -- after the ball, it's an economic free-fall. I had to get lost. That's how I became found. I -

MOHAMMED: Forgive me. I thought this was a business meeting, -

GERALD You need to know where I'm coming from to understand where I'm going -- hopefully with this pretty lady by my side. (winks at JASPORA) I was always into my threads. When you got a body like mine, you want to dress it up proper, special. I subscribed to GQ, but VOGUE and POSE too „cause I was always interested in what the hotties was wearing --I try to be in touch with my female side. (off MOHAMMED"s react) Look, man, I'm getting to the point. Turns out a female acquaintance of mine runs a sweatshop over in East Atlanta and is designing clothes for Us Folks. Because the South is getting a makeover in a big way. I've been consulting on her designs, and using some of my international contacts to create a buzz.

MOHAMMED: So, to cut to the chase, you want Jaspora to be a seamstress?

GERALD : You ever heard of Iman?

MOHAMMED: Missus David Bowie Iman?

GERALD: She was Somali too. Changed the face of fashion, and still could too if she wanted -- „cause you know black don't crack! But she modeled clothes designed by white people, and except for Tommy Hilfiger, white folks don't know how to dress us folks. We need to launch a new line of threads for the New South, the Black South, with an Iman of the New

Millennium -- (pause for effect) You're looking at her.
Jaspora's the shit, she's wet – she's the bombdiggity.
MOHAMMED: You want Jaspora to model?
GERALD: In a word.
MOHAMMED: Are you aligned to a model agency?
GERALD: This a mom-and-pop operation, -
MOHAMMED: How you plan to pay her?
GERALD: There's boocoo cash in the hood. She'll get
paid, I promise you.
MOHAMMED: Promises don't cut it.
GERALD: Relax, man! She's just like Iman -
MOHAMMED: She is NOT. Iman was not Bantu.
Iman was college educated, working on a poli-sci
degree. She wasn't herding goats or cleaning houses
or trying to stay alive in a refugee camp. Jaspora was
a SLAVE.
GERALD: Was. Not is. We're getting out from under.
Jaspora represents us the way we wanna be. That's
actually what we're planning to call our line of
clothing.
MOHAMMED: What?
GERALD: *SLAVE*.

Gerald opens his attache case.

GERALD: (cont'd) I brought along some swatches,
some sketches of a couple ideas, plus we've built a
couple designer samples -
MOHAMMED: That won't be necessary, -

GERALD: Don't shut me down, man. It ain't just me. This is something she wants. It's a dream. Don't be killing dreams, man.

MOHAMMED: Whose dreams? I'm not interested in your dreams! What are you, a child? She's not a toy! She's not a symbol! She's real. (rises) Come on, Jaspora. Let's get outa here.

BETTY: Um, Mohammed? This is her house.

MOHAMMED: This is entirely unprofessional --!!

BETTY: Gerald's all we have. You have to listen.

MOHAMMED: Jaspora, -- (stops, looks at her) Do you really want this?

GERALD: (before she can answer) Look here.

Gerald reveals several kinte patterns used in revolutionary ways. Actually, very good ideas.

GERALD: (cont'd) You're aware of our state flag, and the flag in South Carolina too. The way the crackers keep the Confederate Southern Cross in our faces day in day out, so we can never get away from our past, so we can never get well, never get free. It's a deliberate thang, everybody knows and nobody done shit about it. Well we have.

Gerald shows a Southern Cross, except instead of stars and stripes the pattern is kinte.

GERALD: (cont'd) And it's about fucking time too.

BETTY: Damn. That's pretty rad.

MOHAMMED: You're supposed to wear that?

GERALD: You better believe it. We got hats and football jerseys -- just like FUBU -- for us, by us. But Jaspora is our ace in the hole. She's gonna bring in a whole new way of clothing our bodies, men and women. These traditional robes of hers? Our girl here is gonna show us slave fashion on the real. Gonna be off the hook.

MOHAMMED: This is stupid, -

BETTY: Not really. It's an extension of the way style's been going. Prison garb, baggies, homie tees and khakis, trucker caps. Why not this?

GERALD: Why not go the source? Why not celebrate what slaves actually wear, particularly if it is beautiful? We plan to collaborate with Jaspora -- and her mother -- to be true to the spirit and design of the real roots. We're gonna take this pattern here -

Touches -- too familiarly -- her robe. Betty notices.

GERALD: (cont'd) And we're gonna build off it. Jaspora's a flat-out jaw-dropper. From the bush to Bush Country, gift-wrapped in *kinte*! Ain't that an irony. (off MOHAMMED's react) Don't worry, man. She'll be a partner. We'll put it in writing.

JASPORA: Yes. We'll put it in writing.

MOHAMMED: This is fanciful! This is not real. Minimum wage is real. Hotel service, laundry detail, fast food – that's real. This so-called business is not simply dreaming, it's factually baseless! And unlike the real stuff, there's no parachute, no welfare, no food stamps, no Medicaid. (to BETTY) I can't believe you even entertained this foolishness.

GERALD: Not so fast. (from the attache) I'm not the child you think I am. My lawyer made these up for me. I think you'll find they're satisfactory. I told you, this is a company, and I don't play. Certainly not with other people's dreams, much less my own.

Mohammed reads the paperwork.

GERALD: (cont'd) That's why I walked away from track and field. Sometimes you have to learn to walk away from the table when respect is no longer being served. Gotta show you're able to leave without saying a word.

Betty looks at Gerald strangely.

BETTY: So you gave up running, huh?
GERALD: Yeah.
BETTY: No one pushed you out? No scandal? No controversy?
GERALD: There's more than meets the eye. Everybody says I cheated. But nobody knows how it really went down. The day I won my gold medal, I had a glass shard in my foot. Broke a wineglass the day before outta sheer nervousness. Right through my sock. Hurt every time I stepped, much less sprinted. But I took that pain and used it to run like I never ran before. That glass shard won my gold medal. Not no ephedrine, THG, HGH, anabolic

160

steroid, dihydrotestosterone high. It was that shard. I still got it. I always will.
BETTY: Um. That's not quite true.
GERALD: Were you there?

Betty tugs at Gerald's coat.

BETTY: Can we talk?
GERALD: In a minute.
BETTY: I think now.
GERALD: Don't Bogart me, this is business.
BETTY: I mean business. (off his dismissive react) Are you fucking her? (silence) Is that too real for you?

Mohammed looks up in shock.

GERALD: Betty.
BETTY: It's a simple question.
GERALD: You and me, we didn't have no exclusive. It was one night. I'm surprised you even remember, -
BETTY: Then you are?
MOHAMMED: Betty! Stop.
BETTY: Rather illuminating, isn't it?
MOHAMMED: I'm telling you to stop.
BETTY: You did stalk her, didn't you? Waited on the landing wearing one of your skin-tight shirts and ass-hugging pairs of slacks? Play her like the pimp you are?
GERALD: (flares) Don't call me that!
BETTY: Except I came out first for a smoke. And I was easy. Oh you got a string a ho's!

161

Gerald rises in fury. Mohammed rises and steps between him and Betty, who steps to.

Mother begins to laugh. First a cackle, then a full-fledged donkey bray of a laugh. She even dances a little in a kind of Africanized Teletubbie shuffle.

Jaspora looks at the floor.

Mohammed becomes aware that her robes have also faded.

MOHAMMED: What happened to your robes?
JASPORA: You told me to use the washer/dryer.
MOHAMMED: But -
JASPORA: Your quarters. I used your quarters.
BETTY: (to MOHAMMED) You dumbass. You wrecked her threads.
MOHAMMED: No.
JASPORA: I met Gerald at the washer/dryer.
GERALD: I fished out her robes before they lost all their color. That's how this whole thing got started. Really. She says she don't have an extra pair. I says my friend might make her a new robe. Well, one thing led to another.
BETTY: All roads to lead to fucking.
MOHAMMED: Stop! (silence, then to JASPORA) I'm sorry.
JASPORA: (to MOHAMMED) Hand-wash is best.
MOHAMMED: I didn't know.

BETTY: Slave ways are the best ways sometimes. Even I know that. America is not the be-all end-all. Actually, America can really fuck you up. That's what I was trying to teach her, -

GERALD: She knows already.

MOHAMMED: (disconsolate) Oh my God. I've lost you. I always thought...wished...hoped.... I failed. It's over, isn't it? (struggles to change tone) You have to be careful. There's sexual counseling, I'm not necessarily equipped to advise, but I can tell you there's a lot of danger out there, -

JASPORA: I know.

MOHAMMED: You did -(to GERALD) You did -- use -- a -

GERALD: Cool out. This is a business meeting! I'm no fool. I always wear a raincoat.

MOHAMMED: Forgive me. (he is slightly overcome) I'm sorry, I -

JASPORA: You forget. We were slaves.

MOHAMMED: You don't have to say anything -

JASPORA: We had to live. My Mother -- me -

Mother is massaging her chest -- a bit lasciviously.

JASPORA: (cont"d) The family business. The only thing the Somali let us do. They raped her. She had the baby -- me. She had a hole too, inside. She had pain, and a stink she couldn't stop -

BETTY: A fistula.

JASPORA: Fistula. No one helped. We lived alone. The stink protected us from the Somali men. A doctor came -- finally -- and fixed her. He explained many things. AIDS, disease. He taught me English. He was a very good teacher to me. But Daadab, Kakuma -- (beat) Very bad places.

Mother speaks in her native tongue.

There will be no translation.

JASPORA: (cont'd) We want to live. And when we heard the Voice of America,.... (smiles and cries) We believed.

Mother goes to the bathroom. Plays with the flush.
Gerald packs up his attache.

GERALD: (to JASPORA) We all got our past dishonors. Some you do yourself, some are done unto you. Either way, it's in the past. Let it be. You're free.
MOHAMMED: (to JASPORA) You are. (to BETTY) We've never had this happen before. I can't compare this.
BETTY: Wow. Never heard you say that before.
MOHAMMED: It's new ground. It's -
GERALD: It's the New South.
BETTY: On the real.
MOHAMMED: There's paperwork. You'll need to register with our offices.

GERALD: No biggie.

MOHAMMED: Here's my card.

GERALD: Here's mine. They exchange, very macho. The meeting has ended. Betty approaches Jaspora.

BETTY: I'm sorry I -

JASPORA: Thank you for everything. I wish I had the words to tell you.

BETTY: You speak better than I do! Where'd you learn? TV? You been watching Barack Obama? Alex Trebek?

JASPORA: Mister Rogers.

BETTY: Creepy.

Betty walks to the door. Mohammed about to go too, when Jaspora stops him.

JASPORA: Muhammad?

Gerald notices.

Winks. Heads out.

GERALD: Do what you gotta do. I'm cool as the other side of the pillow.

Betty stares hard at him. They go out to the landing. Mohammed has a hard time looking at Jaspora. He seems on the verge of a nervous attack.

JASPORA: Muhammad, -

MOHAMMED: I can't tell you how sorry I am about your robes -

JASPORA: Muhammad, -

MOHAMMED: I wish you well. Mister McClellan seems to have a workable plan. But if there is anything you wish for that you're not getting, please - - please -- do not hesitate to let me know....

JASPORA: (talk-sings a Mister Rogers song) I HAVE ALWAYS WANTED TO HAVE A NEIGHBOR -

MOHAMMED: Jaspora, -

JASPORA: JUST LIKE YOU, I'VE ALWAYS WANTED TO LIVE IN THE NEIGHBORHOOD WITH YOU

MOHAMMED: What're you --?

JASPORA: SO LET'S MAKE THE MOST OF THIS BEAUTIFUL DAY, SINCE WE'RE TOGETHER WE MIGHT AS WELL SAY, COULD YOU BE MINE, WILL YOU BE MINE, WON'T YOU BE MY NEIGHBOR --? (smiles) I'm learning to sing.

MOHAMMED: Not quite Celine Dion.
JASPORA: You don't like it?
MOHAMMED: I love your voice.
JASPORA: I love the song. (dreamy) This man,....

MOHAMMED: Gerald?

JASPORA: Mister Rogers. I sat in the dark, and cried.
My English. My clothes. But this man was so kind.
His voice. His -- how you call it - (mimes)

MOHAMMED: Coat?

JASPORA: No.

MOHAMMED: Sweater?

JASPORA: Yes. And his songs. They make me feel
that it's okay. Because I have been a slave. But I have
dreams. Even if my English won't let me tell you.

Her smile makes him look down.

MOHAMMED: Your English is beautiful. (to himself)
And I'm a fool. (begins to leave, stops) May I give you
something? (off her smile) They're small.

He hands her his two Homies.

She plays with them.

MOHAMMED: (cont'd) I like the girl. Her coat. I
wonder what's inside.

JASPORA: I like the boy. He has a problem with his
legs?

MOHAMMED: He's been wounded.

JASPORA: They are friends. Aren't they?

MOHAMMED: Very excellent friends.

JASPORA: Thank you, Muhammad.

This time they smile together.

MOHAMMED: (he has to laugh) My mother always washed my clothes for me. Now I have a service do it. One of my clients, a Sudanese Lost Boy, he works there. It was my ignorance. Pure lack of knowledge. Let me pay for your robes -

He pulls out his wallet.

JASPORA: No.
MOHAMMED: But I want to -
JASPORA: You paid me. (holds up the HOMIES) It's a good trade.

Mohammed replaces his wallet.

MOHAMMED: I'll go.
JASPORA: Wait. (winks)

They need to talk. Mohammed nods. Jaspora brings him the shopping bag. Mohammed opens it. Pulls out the terry-cloth robe.

MOHAMMED: You don't like it?
JASPORA: I am not equal. So I shouldn't wear it.
MOHAMMED: Then you must wear it.

Mohammed replaces it in the bag. Gives it back to her.

JASPORA: Muhammad, -
MOHAMMED: You're equal. No matter what.
JASPORA: Even when I'm not?

MOHAMMED: Even then.

She starts to carry it away. Gently, he urges her to place the bag on her head. She sets the bag down.

JASPORA: No. (quotes BETTY) This is how we do things here.

Mother flushes the toilet.

MOHAMMED: Is she all right?
JASPORA: Oh yes.
MOHAMMED: Is the toilet so amazing? The plumbing? The technology? Is that why?
JASPORA: (laughs) It's so WASTEFUL. In Somalia, we never waste water. For anything. Here, you waste everything. When my mother -- or I -- get angry, we waste a little. Because we can.

Mohammed about to speak, instead nods.

JASPORA: (cont'd) But we're not so angry anymore.
MOHAMMED: You can be angry.
JASPORA: We don't need to be.

They are close together.

MOHAMMED: If anything goes wrong, if you need anything at all... Will you...call me?

Jaspora smiles.

OUTSIDE, -

Betty smokes.

GERALD: Come on now.
BETTY: I'm fine.
GERALD: Don't play me.
BETTY: Don't play me.

They're silent.

GERALD: Can I bum one?
BETTY: No.
GERALD: Can I --?
BETTY: No.
GERALD: Will you let me exp--?
BETTY: Shut your meazy. (beat) I'm fine. Whatever. (assumes a professional demeanor) So. Best of luck with your endeavors.
GERALD: Excuse me?
BETTY: Your endeavors. It means do well.
GERALD: I know what it means, -
BETTY: If you mess with babygirl, I'll cut your heart out. And I'll do it too.
GERALD: Don't worry about my endeavors. I'll do it in style. Maybe not according to the rules, but it'll be sweet. I don't like cookie cutter -- I like cookies. First things first, I'll take your girl outa this hellhole, put her up in style. Ain't gonna have no complaints.

BETTY: And the mom? (off his react) Hadn't thought about her, had ya?

GERALD: She can come too!

BETTY: In the end, we all get played. But I don't like getting clowned.

GERALD: Ain't no clowns around here.

BETTY Better not be.

Mohammed opens the door.

MOHAMMED: Excuse me.

GERALD: Excuse me.

Gerald goes inside.

Betty smokes. Mohammed shares the cigarette with her.

MOHAMMED: You all right?

BETTY: Bombdiggity. You?

MOHAMMED: Surprisingly well.

BETTY: Sorry I called you a dumbass.

MOHAMMED: I can't believe I wrecked her robes.

BETTY: Know what? We're both too close.

MOHAMMED: Close is good. We're both too needy.

BETTY: Are they gonna be all right?

MOHAMMED: I don't know.

They go.

Betty stops.

BETTY: You said you were one of them.
MOHAMMED: We should get going.

Neither moves.

BETTY One of them?
MOHAMMED: I meant new. Without belongings.
(shrugs) Absolute rock bottom.
BETTY: No way to go but up?
MOHAMMED: Is this up?
BETTY: (looks around) Yeah. Bullshit as it may be.
This is up.

They share the cigarette.

MOHAMMED: The Indomitable Lions.
BETTY: Excuse me?
MOHAMMED: My home team. Football.
BETTY: You're from Detroit?
MOHAMMED: The other kind of football. But it feels
like a world away.
BETTY It's right there.

She touches his chest. She almost pulls away, doesn't.

Mohammed starts to SNEEZE. Before he can, --

*Betty SNEEZES. Actually she finishes the sneeze he
started.*

Silence as they recognize what just happened.

Slowly, each smiles.

INSIDE, Gerald reacts as if he's just won the Gold medal.

GERALD: YES! How do you like me now? What's my name? CAN YOU DIG IT???

As he preens, Jaspora and Mother speak in their language.

MOTHER: You picked the wrong guy.
JASPORA: We have to move forward. We're in America. Move or you get left behind.
MOTHER: He loves you.
JASPORA: Gerald?
MOTHER: Not Gerald.
JASPORA: I love him too. So?
GERALD: (clueless) Hey. Guys. Speak English, huh?

They ignore him.

JASPORA: Take off your clothes.
MOTHER: Why?
GERALD: Ladies? English!
JASPORA: Take them off. There's no going back. So we move forward. And we do it now.

Jaspora goes into Gerald's attache, pulls out new clothes. Tosses Mother one of the new SLAVE fashions.

GERALD: Hey. Wow. What's going on?

They speak English. Accented, but growingly comfortable.

JASPORA: Don't get excited, Gerald. (smiles) We're in business.
MOTHER: No more cows, Gerald.

As the ladies take off their clothes, -

CAST: BUT NOTHING IS AS BEAUTIFUL AS
WHEN SHE BELIEVES WHEN SHE BELIEVES
WHEN SHE BELIEVES WHEN SHE BELIEVES
WHEN SHE BELIEVES....

<u>SCENE 4</u>

The lobby of The Four Corners Hotel.

Gerald enters.

Glenna serves him at the front desk.

GLENNA: Welcome to the Four Corners.
GERALD: I have a reservation.
GLENNA: For one?
GERALD: Actually, three.

Gerald turns as Jaspora enters, Mother by her side. Both wear the new SLAVE fashions -- Africanized hip-hop, gangsta tribal. Both move regally, both turn heads.

Jaspora smiles at Glenna.

GLENNA: Three. (searching) Mister McClellan.
GERALD: Bangbang McClellan.

Drops his credit card in front of her.

GERALD: (cont'd) (to JASPORA) They got real nice
rooms, baby.
JASPORA: Big TV?
GERALD: Big as you please. (to GLENNA) Right?
GLENNA: Absolutely.
MOTHER: Cow's milk?
GLENNA: Excuse me?
GERALD: The lady likes her milk fresh.
GLENNA: Of course.

Glenna sets to the paperwork.

MUZAK "When You Wish Upon a Star."

GERALD: This'll work till we get our offices together.
We can take meetings, have room service bring food
up. About as far from the bush as you've ever been!
They got big bathtubs and big beds, and oh yeah they
got these thick terry cloth robes for every guest to
keep! (off JASPORA"s nod) I'm glad you mentioned
this place. You come a long way, baby. Me too. And
little by little, the South's coming along with us!
Whether they want to or not. (winks at GLENNA)
Ain't that right?

Glenna looks up, recognizes Jaspora.

JASPORA: Hi Neighbor.

As she stares back, -

CAST: WHEN SHE BELIEVES WHEN SHE
BELIEVES....IN ME

As the cast plays to the end, -

*Betty helps Mohammed put on a NuSouth kinte
confederate flag shirt.*

As he feels his heart, -

END OF PLAY

THE WALLOWA PROJECT

By

Oliver Mayer
In collaboration with the Son of
Semele Ensemble

WALLOWA: The Vanishing of Maude LeRay

Production

Written by Oliver Mayer, in collaboration with The
Company
Conceived and Directed by Don Boughton
Scenic Design by Sarah Krainin
Lighting Design by Barbara Kallir
Sound Design by Bob Blackburn
Costume Design by Daniella Langford
Video Design by Matthew McCray
Music by Gabriel Liebeskind, Matthew McCray and
Alexander Wright
Choreography by Sharyn Gabriel
Dramaturgy by Bryan Davidson
Artwork by Esther Choi
Stage Managed by Kyle Roberts
Production Management by Yolanda Hester &
Matthew McCray

Cast

The roles of:

**Maude, Howard, Dispatcher, Ranger, Michael, Fred,
Tuck, Ash, Honey, Alex, Carrie, Marty, Shock Jock,
Crows, Gnats, Feral Dog, Coyote, Bear, Rattlesnake,
Salmon, Fox**

were played by:

*Sarah Boughton, Sharyn Gabriel, *Daniel Getzoff, Gabriel Liebeskind, Gina Manziello, *Matthew McCray, Alex Smith, Dee Sudik, Diana Payne, *Alexander Wells, *Jonathan CK Williams and *Alexander Wright.

appearing courtesy of Actors' Equity Association

The world premiere occurred on April 8, 2011 at Son of Semele Ensemble, Los Angeles, under the direction of Don Boughton.

PROLOGUE

Dense forest.

Sound of distant thunder.

Lightning, stretching across horizon, morphs into the image of flying crow.

Flashes of lights scurry across the forest floor.

FIGURES in silhouette rise in a circle. They dance, sing.

Sound of a truck crashing into tree. Tires spin, engine grinds to a halt.

FIGURES freeze.

Silence. Blackout.

ACT ONE
SCENE ONE
CALLOUT

Crackle of two-way radio. A cell phone descends from the grid. "......" Then another and another ....

<u>Voice Over.</u>

DISPATCHER: Callout. S&R. Missing hunter. Female. Stage at Two Colors Trailhead, repeat Two Colors, Eagle Creek Road. High angle, night gear. Respond on Code 9. Case 373.

Lights full reveal a broken line of figures facing the audience.

They place hats on heads.

ALL: See ya there.

Everyone gathers around the SHERIFF.

SHERIFF: Gather around. Maps, GPSes, team bags – Show me….And orange gear, it's hunting season.
TUCK: Why not just put a target on our backs.
MEL: How about antler caps?
TUCK: (meaning the opposite) Gotta love the AFH.
FRED: (translates for HONEY) Another Effing Hunter.

Honey shows Sheriff her orange gear.

SHERIFF: Good. Radio channels to "9" – we'll switch around often so pay attention. If this goes on long, the

Media will be listening. Pairings: Mel/Ash, Honey, where's...okay, Fred. Tuck with me.

FRED: Great.

TUCK: Ready to serve, Ready to save.

SHERIFF: Look, let's get this out in the open right now. I may be new to the job and I may not know you all that well yet, but I'm making no apologies. I'm calling the shots. If anybody doesn't like it, now's the time to speak your piece. (silence) Okay. Check your maps, the LKP is here.

HONEY: The L whatdya say?

FRED: The Last Known Point.

MEL: The Last Known Point.

SHERIFF: That's where the trailer and SUV went down. The PLS – (looks at HONEY) -- Place Last Seen – is over 4 miles away, here...We're moving southeasterly from the border of O'Brien Creek. Trails first, think what she would do; if we have to, we'll back track and beat the bushes. I don't have to remind you, this terrain is treacherous. It's cold and wet and slicker than snot. Now the bad news: she was last seen at Friday noon.

Hub-bub.

MICHAEL: So, when does the clock start – then or now?

SHERIFF: Between us – it starts now. We're giving some leeway here. It's obvious that the trail is stale. Can't depend on the hounds or aircraft. It's all on us. One last thing: she's 76 years old.

More hub-bub.

Questions – "Does she have water?" "What is she wearing?" etc.

SHERIFF: We're working on it! (they keep asking) Focus! Sooner than later, let's bring her in from the cold.

SCENE TWO
INTERROGATION/LOST

Howard, arm set and bandaged, sits with the Sheriff. Dispatcher outside.

HOWARD: Swallowed by the monster.
SHERIFF: Monster?
HOWARD: Swallowed everything but me.
SHERIFF: That worked out well.
HOWARD: Why aren't we up there?
SHERIFF: Search and Rescue Team is already there scouring the area.
HOWARD: Then let's go.

Howard rises. Sheriff doesn't move.

SHERIFF: Monster. How?
HOWARD: All mouth.
SHERIFF: And it swallowed Maude.

HOWARD: And everything! Trees and rocks and grass and sky.

SHERIFF: Pretty huge monster.

HOWARD: It would have to be.

SHERIFF: If Maude is dead, then what's the rush?

HOWARD: I didn't say she was dead! I said she was swallowed! (slight pause) I shouldn't' t have said anything.

SHERIFF: I'm glad you did. Have another cup of coffee. (quietly, to DISPATCHER) Call the Deputy.

HOWARD: Why?

SHERIFF: Sit down.

HOWARD: Why the cops?

SHERIFF: Because this is sounding more and more like foul play.

HOWARD: What the hell are you talking about?

SHERIFF: Your state of mind. Lose your wife up there, don't really quite know where. Injured just badly enough to deflect suspicion.

HOWARD: Suspicion of what? We've been married forever!

SHERIFF: Precisely. Why'd you kill her?

Howard rises in anger.

Dispatcher gets between him and the Sheriff.

HOWARD: I will have your badge.

SHERIFF: Every hour she's up there reduces her chances of survival. Every wrong hunch, every mistaken clue. Every distorted dream can throw us off the scent. And I hold you responsible.

HOWARD: So do I.

SHERIFF: (after a moment, to DISPATCHER) Hold off on that call – for now.

HOWARD: At least it's not too cold up there this time of year.

SHERIFF: Cold coming, rain, sleet. What's she wearing?

HOWARD: Cotton.

SHERIFF: All cotton?

HOWARD: She likes organic fiber, what do you want me to say?

SHERIFF: Something to give me a clue about what choices she might make up there. Otherwise you're wasting my time. I mean, hell, this is your *wife*!

Howard's hurt arms throbs.

HOWARD: Dammit!

Maude appears, walking through the forest. She speaks only to him.

MAUDE: Your arm?

HOWARD: Your shoe is untied.

MAUDE: Oh God. These laces hate me. Well, they do! I'm too tired to bother.

HOWARD: If you break a foot falling down because you didn't tie your shoe, then we're really stuck.

MAUDE: I need a drink. (off his react) Of *water*.

HOWARD: Left it in the camper. Couple of geniuses we are, huh?

MAUDE: We?

HOWARD: Come on, gotta keep moving!

MAUDE: We've been going all morning!

HOWARD: Ranger Station can't be that far!

MAUDE: You said that an hour ago!

HOWARD: I remember it just down from that campsite!

MAUDE: You can't remember the names of your own daughters!

HOWARD: We're not lost!

SHERIFF: Howard? Howard?

HOWARD: (to SHERIFF) We were really lost before I realized. (to HIMSELF) I'm still lost.

MAUDE: I can't go on!

HOWARD: Okay, okay. How about this? You rest here. I find help and send up here to get you?

MAUDE: Half okay. There's no telling how long you'll be. I'm going to back track to the camper. (cutting off his protests) You still need to get to the doctor. They'll have to drive you to Enterprise or Baker City, who knows? That'll take till evening. At least this way I'll have water, food, the camper in case it rains. (touches his hand) I'll be fine.

HOWARD: Some holiday.

MAUDE: Everything that could go wrong did.

SHERIFF: (to HOWARD) What were you thinking?

MAUDE: (to HOWARD) You weren't. (slight pause) Neither was I.

HOWARD: Naw, it's on me. How can I make this up to you?

MAUDE: Call the girls. Carrie anyway, let her know we're okay.

HOWARD: I don't need her needling me.

MAUDE: Then Margo.

HOWARD: Margo's too busy to care one way or the other.

MAUDE: Okay, they don't have to know.

Neither moves. Both look out at the vast darkness.

MAUDE: I've missed these mountains.

HOWARD: (to SHERIFF) She loved these mountains.

SHERIFF: Love 'em how?

HOWARD: Their history?

SHERIFF: You mean the Nez Perce? Chief Joseph? The Nee Mee Poo?

MAUDE: (corrects him) Nu Mee Poo.

SHERIFF: Snake River Canyon? Evil Knievel?

HOWARD: No, personal history. She had a life, before me. She used to come here.

Maude smiles.

HOWARD: She was a biker chick. She'd bring me here on the ass end of a, what was it,...?

MAUDE: Triumph Twin 650. Cherry.

HOWARD: She used to ride up here in the Wallowas. This was her place. (to MAUDE) Once this is all over, we'll go a long hike.
MAUDE: May be my last chance.
HOWARD: For what? I don't know about you, but I'm planning on living forever.
MAUDE: Let's get through today first.

They share a moment. Then he starts off.

MAUDE: Wait! The keys!
HOWARD: Ooops. I don't got 'em.
MAUDE: Check your pockets.
HOWARD: Nothing. Here, check this one, I can't get it.
MAUDE: Nothing! Oh God, did you drop them on the trail?

Obnoxious CROW CAWS.
HOWARD: What was that?
MAUDE: Forest noises.
HOWARD: Sounded like some kind of monster.
MAUDE: More like crow.
HOWARD: Crow?

She points above. As he looks, she feels her pocket.

MAUDE: Ooops. Guess what I just found.

Jangles keys.

SHERIFF: Crow.

Howard pays him no mind, staring at Maude.

HOWARD: One last thing. Tie that shoe.

Maude ties it. Models the result.

HOWARD: Looking good.
MAUDE: (sexily) Give ya something to think about.
Now go.
HOWARD: I'm gone.

Maude sits alone.

MAUDE: (to herself)
A MIGHTY FORTRESS IS MY GOD
A BULWARK NEVER FAILING....

Howard turns back to the Sheriff.

HOWARD: I got to tell my girls. What do I tell my
girls?
SHERIFF: Tell them we're doing everything we can.

Dispatcher enters with a set of hotel keys.

SHERIFF: We'll put you up at the Oregon Trail Motel
in town. Now do us a favor and stay out of the way.
We'll be in touch as soon as we know something.
Clear your head and we'll talk again, later.

HOWARD: Thanks.
SHERIFF: Howard? No monster.
HOWARD: That's what you think.

Howard shuffles out.

Sheriff watches him go.

Maude looks at her shoes, already beginning to untie.

CROW CAWS overhead.

MAUDE: Shut yer trap!

She breathes. Shrugs.

MAUDE: No bird. No man. No house. No kids.
(smiles) Nothing.

Sounds of running water.

MAUDE: Thirsty.

Maude moves towards the sound, exits.

A moment later, she returns, laces undone.

The murder of crows descends, peck at her shoes, steal them.

Maude steals them back, exits.

Howard returns, in confusion and terror.

HOWARD: Maude!

<u>SCENE THREE</u>
<u>READY TO ROLL</u>

Search and Rescue team members spread out in pairs.

The last pair remains. FRED ready to go. HONEY continues to pack slowly. She wears a denim vest and a **SATAN SUCKS** *cap.*

HONEY: Ready to rock?
FRED: I am.
HONEY: Well I'm not.
FRED: Is that all you're bringing?

HONEY: Don't like to be weighted down.
FRED: Gonna be cold.
HONEY: I like a little weather.
FRED: You're gonna get it. Even the bears will be wearing long johns tonight.
HONEY: What was her name again? Maude?
FRED: (pointedly) Soon as you're packed, we'll start up.
HONEY: How's life at **Charbucks**?
FRED: Wonderful.
HONEY: I know the secret.
FRED: Secret?

HONEY: Why Starbucks rules the world. (a beat) You burn the beans.
FRED: We do not.
HONEY: You release the chemicals. Might as well be meth.
FRED: Starbucks is a progressive institution! Plus I can't help it if the product is addictive.
HONEY: Hey, I used to love drugs. Didya bring any?
FRED: Drugs?
HONEY: Coffee!
FRED: Sorry.

Honey hums "Amazing Grace" as she starts moving. Wrong-footed, he follows her. They reach a fork in the trail.

He chooses a direction.

HONEY: Why this way? We're just gonna get wet going through here.
FRED: What would Maude have done? Would she have taken the easy trail?
HONEY: She was thirsty.
FRED: Bennett Creek's this way. Let's go this direction.
HONEY: Me first.

They go.

SCENE FOUR
DOUBTS

Maude wanders through, still confident, but more frustrated. Invisible.

Sheriff pours a cup of Starbucks coffee for the Receptionist.

DISPATCHER: You trying to bribe me for an opinion?

SHERIFF: Will it work?

DISPATCHER: Memory is a slippery organ.

SHERIFF: Is that a come-on?

DISPATCHER: It exists in different parts of the brain at the same time. The connections are personal. What makes sense to me might not make sense at all to you.

SHERIFF: That's the truth.

DISPATCHER: To forget is to be human.

SHERIFF: Then Howard is definitely human. Can you believe this guy? He's so excited to bag an elk, he gets here two days early, but he gets lost. He's got a new crossbow he doesn't know how to use. And he's got a brand new camo suit for the occasion, but he's not wearing it!

DISPATCHER: Sounds sweet.

SHERIFF: Fishy, more like. He cracks the axle, tries to take off the ATV but the trailer tips. He busts his arm. They spend the first night in the cab. Apparently there's provisions enough in there for a week. But no, the next day they start walking – with nothing! I mean, what the hell?

DISPATCHER: You said his arm was broken.

SHERIFF: So?

DISPATCHER: You ever had a broken arm? Hurts like hellfire.

SHERIFF: (grumbles) They split up mid-way. You never split up! Today he's found by hunters. He gets his arm fixed. Now he finally reports her missing. A full day has passed! I mean, hell, that's half the allotted time for Search and Rescue! And this terrain! He's gotta know that a quarter mile here is denser and more unpredictable than just about anywhere. Where's his brain?

DISPATCHER: You ever had an accident?

SHERIFF: I'm a very good driver.

DISPATCHER: Well it's no fun. I remember my first.

SHERIFF: You've had more than one?

DISPATCHER: Everything was floating. I remember I put my hand out to prepare for impact, and it went right through the dashboard, clear past the radio. I came home, sat on the toilet with an un-dialed phone in one hand and a doughnut in the other, and it wasn't till my cats came over to me that I realized that something was wrong. Shock. Trauma. Give the man a break and don't jump to any conclusions till we find the wife.

SHERIFF: That's your opinion?

DISPATCHER: That's my story and I'm sticking to it.

Tuck appears at the door. Sheriff rises to join him.

SHERIFF: I hear ya.

SCENE FIVE
WILDERNESS CLAUTROPHOBIA

Maude, increasingly disjointed, confused, in sliding frames of wilderness as if conceived by the artist Joseph Cornell.

SCENE SIX
SEARCHING BY SENSE

SIMULTANEOUSLY, two rescuers search for Maude in the forest. It is slow going, wet. They talk as they work; if anything it adds to their focus.

MEL: "If a man says something in the woods and there are no women there, is he still wrong?" I'd say pretty much without a doubt that was the best one-liner of the whole episode. I mean, it's SURVIVOR REDEMPTION ISLAND, not Shakespeare.
ASH: Ugh! How can you watch that stuff?
MEL: Guess I'm hooked on reality.
ASH: That's not real.
MEL: As real as your "premonitions."
ASH: Excuse me?

Mel reacts as if she didn't hear her. Ash stops, closes her eyes.

MEL: Ash! You all right?
ASH: Something just went through me.
MEL: These leaves and branches get pretty sharp.
ASH: No! A feeling. (looks up) You see that? Through the talus?
MEL: Looks like a cave.

ASH: Looks like a blow-hole. An upside-down mound.

MEL: Whatever. Good place to get out the rain. But you'd need climbing equipment just to even dream of getting up there. Never happen.

ASH: I got a feeling.

MEL: And I'm just being real.

Mel sees something underfoot.

MEL: Whoa!

ASH: What?

MEL: Wow.

ASH: Talk to me!

MEL: I always wondered where these ended up.

She holds up an old sock.

MEL: You know, when you do a wash and end, Up with one sock AWOL? Where do they go? Here, I guess.

ASH: Think it's hers?

MEL: Big feet.

Mel stretches the sock to show its size.

ASH: Maybe it belonged to Big Foot!

MEL: Maybe she's with Big Foot and Sasquatch and the Loch Ness Monster washing clothes, wondering where the other sock went.

Mel goes silent.

ASH: What, Mel?
MEL: Wish I knew who the hell she was.
ASH: Is.
MEL: Is.

Ash continues to look up; Mel continues to look underfoot.

SCENE SEVEN
THE BRIDGE OF CHAIRS

Maude attempts to traverse the forest, through streams and underbrush, created by chairs. Eventually she makes her way up into a kind of nest.

SCENE EIGHT

Sheriff and Tuck struggle through underbrush.

TUCK: Hear that?
SHERIFF: Oh no. Are you kidding me?

Howard appears in the distance, oblivious, hacking through underbrush.

TUCK: He's contaminating the trail. Didn't you tell him –?
SHERIFF: Of course I did! He's a damn fool. (calls out) Howard! (no response) Howard! (to TUCK) I bet he did this deliberately.

TUCK: Did what?

SHERIFF: We'll lose the rest of day apprehending him, escorting him down the mountain. And I bet that's just what he wants.

TUCK: What? You think he meant to lose her?

SHERIFF: You ever been in a bad marriage? (TUCK has) Your mind goes all kinds of places. Wrong as it sounds, you wish she'd just get lost somewhere and never come back. Meanwhile, she's wishing you dead too.

TUCK: You've thought a lot about this.

SHERIFF: I'm not saying he did it consciously. But actions speak. If you loved somebody, would you leave her alone up here?

Sheriff grimly starts towards Tuck.

TUCK: Wait. Let me deal with him.

SHERIFF: He might get physical.

TUCK: He doesn't scare me.

SHERIFF: I'm right here if you need me. And I'm not afraid to use my gun.

TUCK: Keep it holstered, thank you.

Tuck approaches Howard, who seems as lost as Lear on the heath.

TUCK: Howard?

HOWARD: I thought you guys had to quit.

TUCK: Only officially.

HOWARD: (RE: SHERIFF) What's his problem?

TUCK: He's new around here. Everything is by the book for him. But he's not the worst guy in the world.
HOWARD: Bastard wants me off the mountain.
TUCK: Probably a good idea. You're liable to get lost again, and that won't help us find Maude.
HOWARD: But I know her best. How she thinks. I know where she keeps her secret stuff.
TUCK: Secrets?
HOWARD: Boxes of photos she keeps under the bed. Stuff from before. People I never knew.
TUCK: I thought you guys were married forever.
HOWARD: You never know it all. (slight pause) I think she met somebody up here.
TUCK: What?
HOWARD: Maybe an old boyfriend. Or a new one.
TUCK: Wouldn't it be easier to meet at a bar?
HOWARD: Nothing easy about Maude. (growingly lost) I'll never know who those people were.
TUCK: Which people?
HOWARD: The ones in the photos! The ones before me. Do you know what I mean?
TUCK: I do.

They sit together.

TUCK: I'm divorced. Pretty recent. We didn't fight. One day she said she was done, and when I tried to argue, I realized I didn't have a very good argument. I let her go. I saved some people up here last year, and something happened to me. I left something up here, lost it like you lose a set of keys, and I just don't know how to be with anyone anymore.

HOWARD: But you found the people?

TUCK: I did.

HOWARD: Maybe it was a trade.

TUCK: Maybe.

They watch as the Sheriff approaches.

HOWARD: He thinks I killed her.

TUCK: Yeah.

HOWARD: Did I?

TUCK: Come on, Howard. Let's get you off this mountain.

They all go, watching their every step.

SCENE NINE
QUANTUM ENTANGLEMENTS

Maude in the forest.

Howard in a motel room, sitting and examining a map.

Maude examines her body by hand.

There is a delayed mirror effect. Based on her touch, but with a lag, Howard becomes aware of parts of his own body.

Eventually he stands.

HOWARD: Maude.

Maude zeroes in on a particular spot on her body. She goes to the place it takes her – memory, sensation.

In delayed fashion, Howard feels something zeroing in on his body.

HOWARD: (collapses) Maude.

Maude stops the self-examination. She becomes aware of the world outside her body – the forest, the ground, the sky.

Howard returns to the map. He intimately fingers areas of it.

Maude becomes aware of something touching her temples. It starts to rain.

MAUDE: Howard. (to the forest) Howard. (to the sky) Howard.

Howard stares at the map in frustration. Finally he pushes it away.

HOWARD: Where?
MAUDE: Here!

Maude uncovers a TATTOO, heretofore hidden beneath clothing.

MAUDE: Right here. (examines it) Part tree, part cloud, part sun, part water, part mountain.

It rains harder.

Howard begins to become aroused. He is not coarse about it, but he experiences the beginnings of a fantasy with an image of his wife, most likely from the past.

A knock at the door.

Howard scrambles, reverie broken.

Howard lets in CARRIE, then MARTY.

Marty embraces Howard. Carrie just stares at him.

Blackout on them.

The rain pours down.

Maude receives it, arms out, mouth open.

The talus starts to slip away.

She grabs hold of the mountain, the tree limbs.

The ground slips out under her feet.

She is left hanging.

MAUDE: HOWARD!!!!

SCENE TEN

Motel Room. Carrie turns on the radio. Static until SHOCK JOCK speaks.

SHOCK JOCK: And this really burns me up, People! So the Nez Perce Indian Tribe is angling to buy sizeable properties all around Wallowa. Why? They want us out. They hate our guts!

Marty turns it off.

MARTY: How can you listen to that?
CARRIE: It's either that or the Holy Rollers. Or Rush.

MARTY: How about nothing?

A moment of tense silence. Carrie begins to hum, then sing:

CARRIE: A MIGHTY FORTRESS IS OUR GOD, A BULLWARK –

MARTY: Really?
CARRIE: I don't like the silence. I need activity.
MARTY: God! You're just like Dad.
CARRIE: It's Mom's song.
MARTY: One of her songs. That whole Christian thing is –
CARRIE: Is what?

MARTY: It's just not the way I hear Mom.
CARRIE: Well I do. It's the Battle Hymn of the Reformation! Martin Luther? Salvation comes not from good deeds but as a gift of God's grace through faith. (MARTY just shrugs) It's beautiful! And Mom sang it to me.
MARTY: Okay. Fine.

Silence. Marty begins to hum, then to sing the Rolling Stones song:

MARTY: KIDS ARE DIFFERENT TODAY, I HEAR EVERY MOTHER SAY....

CARRIE: Must you?

MARTY: SHE GOES RUNNING TO THE SHELTER /OF HER MOTHER'S LITTLE HELPER --

CARRIE: Shut up, Marty!
MARTY: Sorry. That's just the way I hear Mom.
CARRIE: Well stop.
MARTY: Then we'll hear her in silence. Okay? Fine.

Carrie can't take the silence, exits. Marty remains, begins to hum.

SCENE ELEVEN
TRIANGLES

Maude in the forest.

205

The forest hums an ambient hum.

She picks it up. Turns it into "Amazing Grace" -- then blows it off.

She goes in and around obstacles, cannot seem to find a way out.

She is beset by GNATS.

They drive her into a clump of rocks. Then they fade away.

She realizes her purse is gone.

She meets a FERAL DOG.
MAUDE: Oh Good Lord.

The Dog growls.

She picks up a rock.

MAUDE: What are you looking at?

The Dog growls.

She growls back.

The Dog protects the CARCASS of a dead ELK.

She picks up a stick.

MAUDE: Nice doggie.

The Dog jumps at her, misses.

She throws the stick. The Dog chases after it.

She faces the carcass of the elk. She moves toward it.

The odor is overwhelming.

She stays there anyway.

She enters the carcass – it feels warm and good.

The earth collapses around her. Lifts her up, then sucks her in.

SCENE TWELVE
CALLING OFF
Sheriff stands in front of the search and rescue teams.

SHERIFF: Gather up….Okay. It's 50 hours from the the first call. You know what's coming: If not found, shut it down.

A chorus of disapproval.

SHERIFF: I know. It hurts. It feels like we failed. But we didn't; anyway, we're not to judge. Go to Scripture: "Judge not, that you be not judged." It's not for us to say. (adopts a tone of eulogy) I hear the woman – Maude – was a good Christian woman. Mother, wife, good neighbor. And I hear she loved these mountains.

Commotion. Howard jostles his way to the front.

HOWARD: Are you eulogizing her? Don't!
SHERIFF: Shut up!
TUCK: Let him speak.
ASH: Tuck!
HOWARD: Just because "she's of a certain age" people are supposed to disappear? You're giving up because at 70 she's close to death anyway? My wife's got more life in her than any of you. She lights up like a flame! I look at Maude, and I see her just the way she was when we first met. If you saw her the way I do, you wouldn't be giving up on her.
HONEY: How do you see her?
HOWARD: Tough. She applied for a job at my company as a truck driver. The guys figured she was there for a receptionist position, she had to show them her truck-driving license. Even then, nobody believed her, she had to prove she could drive a cement truck. By now they called me outa my office. I looked at her and she looked pretty cute. So I got in the cab with her and she didn't miss a beat. Put that beast in gear, took charge, like she was born for it.That's Maude. Thirty years gone by and I can still she her young as any of you. So don't you put her in the past tense. Don't you make her invisible.

SHERIFF: Look. No one is giving up. We'll keep a Ranger on duty in the campground to interview every back country visitor who comes through here. We'll be watchful for any clue.

Howard backs away and off, looking lost.

Pause, as he speaks to his Search and Rescue team.

SHERIFF: She will be found. But we just have to face reality. She's gone to God now.

END ACT ONE

ACT TWO

SCENE 1
MAUDE IN THE MAW

Maude within the maw of the dead animal.

The earth seems to belch and fart.

Maude is revealed from within, in a fetal position.

Chorus moves around her, as if inside the maw with her.

MAUDE: Where am I?
CHORUS 1: The Monster's belly.
MAUDE: Monster?

CHORUS 2: Very big monster.

CHORUS 1: It eats everything in sight.

CHORUS 2: Ate all the little animals –

CHORUS 1: And the big animals –

CHORUS 2: And the People –

CHORUS 1: Even the rocks and trees.

Coyote enters.

COYOTE: Everything but me.

MAUDE: Who are you?

COYOTE: Just folks. (offers his paw) Coyote.

MAUDE: Why didn't you get e't?

COYOTE: I move too fast. Think too much.

MAUDE: Then why are you here?

COYOTE: Got lonely. I missed my People.

Coyote greets and high fives the Chorus.

CHORUS 1: Bear.

CHORUS 2: Rattlesnake.

CHORUS 3: Salmon.

CHORUS 4: Fox.

COYOTE: Missed you guys.

BEAR: Ate all of us – and some of us don't taste so good.

SALMON: Speak for yourself!

MAUDE: No, this isn't right. This is not me.

COYOTE: Don't be upset, I'm sure you taste delicious.

MAUDE: Stop!

Maude begins to circle the edges of the maw, looking for an opening.

RATTLESNAKE: What's she doing?
SALMON: Swimming upstream.
MAUDE: How do you get out?
CHORUS: Out?
COYOTE: (shrugs) Good question. Hadn't really thought about it too much. I mean, face it, one way or another, you're gonna get eaten.
MAUDE: Don't say that! It's eat or be eaten!
CHORUS: (correcting her) Eat **and** be eaten.

COYOTE: Not or.
MAUDE: Get me out of here!
COYOTE: Out, huh?
MAUDE: Yes, out!
COYOTE: How would I do that?

Maude looks for an answer.

MAUDE: What's in your pouch?
COYOTE: This?

Coyote removes items.

COYOTE: Fire starter kit.
CHORUS: Oooh.
COYOTE: Pitch.

CHORUS: Aaah.
COYOTE: And five stone knives.

Maude rises.

MAUDE: You can start a fire.
COYOTE: I could?
MAUDE: Then cut us out of here!
COYOTE: Ambitious.
MAUDE: Don't you want to get out?
COYOTE: I just got here. (embraces CHORUS) Not
so bad. All my friends.
MAUDE: But what about your life?
COYOTE: My what?

MAUDE: Your life!
COYOTE: What do you mean, life?
MAUDE: I mean – life! – credit card bills! Blood
pressure meds! Wal-Mart runs.
CHORUS: Let it go.
MAUDE: Let it go? There's shirts in the washer! Next
week it's Margot's birthday! The Explorer needs new
tires!
CHORUS: Let it go.
MAUDE: I won't!
CHORUS: Why not?
MAUDE: If I do,... What else is there? (no response)
This is who I am!
CHORUS: What is?

MAUDE: ME! (struggling) My faith! (no response) A MIGHTY FORTRESS IS OUR GOD/A BULWARK NEVER FAILING –

She chokes.

Chorus SINGS in its own language.

MAUDE: I am my children. My husband. My church.
COYOTE: I thought you were just folks like us. (off her react) People.
MAUDE: You're not people.

The Chorus reacts as one.

CHORUS: We're not?

COYOTE: Are we so different? Really?
MAUDE: If you're people like me, then cut me out of here.
BEAR: Maybe she's right.
FOX: She's people and she wants out.
RATTLESNAKE: Maybe we do too.
MAUDE: Cut me out of here!!
CHORUS: (correcting her) Us.
MAUDE: All right, us!
COYOTE: How?
MAUDE: Start a fire.
COYOTE: Here in the belly?
MAUDE: (nods) Then cut out its heart.
COYOTE: Pretty big heart. What if the stone breaks?

MAUDE: You have five knives!

COYOTE: It's a heart. It's not easy to cut. Plus it's connected to lots of other stuff. There will be repercussions.

MAUDE: I want my life.

COYOTE: You sure about this? (silence) There are only so many exits. (looks to CHORUS) How shall we go out? Through the nose?

CHORUS: Snotty.

COYOTE: The mouth?

CHORUS: Bad breath.

COYOTE: The ears?

CHORUS: Earwax.

COYOTE: The anus?

CHORUS: Shit!

MAUDE: Do it.

COYOTE: Must we?

MAUDE: Yes.

CHORUS: You would pass through the ass of the monster, just to get back to what you call your life?

MAUDE: A thousand times yes.

COYOTE: Okay. Then find something to burn.

Maude trips over bones. Picks one up.

MAUDE: Burn this.

Chorus reacts in horror.

COYOTE: Oh no. Mustn't do that.

CHORUS: Bones!
COYOTE: Can't burn them. Can't sell 'em.
CHORUS: Ancestors.

*Maude looks for anything to burn, including her own
meager possessions.*

MAUDE: There has got to be something!

*Gives them to Coyote – her ID, photos, jewelry, socks –
anything now excess.*

COYOTE: These'll burn. (uses flint) Gonna get smoky.

*Coyote creates fire from flint, summons it, for a moment
looking like Jimmi Hendrix coaxing fire from his electric
guitar.*

MAUDE: Burn, baby, burn.

*The inside of the monster is now roiling and belching, in a
fiery glow.*

COYOTE: I'm going to start cutting the heart. Now be
prepared to get out through any opening that you
can.

*Coyote addresses the heart of the monster, which seems to
be everywhere and also invisible.*

MAUDE: What are you doing?

COYOTE: Duh! Cutting out the heart!
MAUDE: Where?
COYOTE: Everywhere!

Coyote slices and hacks away at air.

COYOTE: Told ya, it's a big heart!

The knife breaks.

COYOTE: Uh-oh.

Tosses the first knife.

MAUDE: Knife Number Two.

This time Coyote addresses a tiny point in the palm of its own paw.

MAUDE: What are you doing?
COYOTE: Cutting out the heart!
MAUDE: Where?
COYOTE: See the lifeline? (shows his palm) The Monster's shifty!

Coyote cuts till the blade breaks.

COYOTE: I knew this would happen.

Tosses blade.

COYOTE: Blade Number Three.

Now Coyote begins to cut down actual Chorus Members, horribly.

MAUDE: What are you doing?!!!
COYOTE: What do you think? Cutting out the heart!

Another blade breaks.

COYOTE: Uh-oh. Only two left.

Picks up Number Four, and continues to hack at Chorus Members.

MAUDE: Stop!
COYOTE: Too late.

Number Four breaks.

COYOTE: Last one.

Coyote takes the last blade and turns on her.

MAUDE: What are you doing?
COYOTE: I'm cutting out the heart.
MAUDE: Get away.
COYOTE: You want out. This is how.
MAUDE: I'm not the monster.
COYOTE: You're not. You're the monster's heart.

Coyote enters her via the mouth.

In so doing, Coyote carves out her teeth with his blade.

She SCREAMS, suddenly now without a voice.

COYOTE: (digging with the blade)
The...last...stubborn...chord...!!!

An EXPLOSION.

The roof and walls of the belly fall away.

Chorus scrambles through the openings made.

COYOTE: Come on, People!

Maude stands still, holding her mouth.

Coyote is the last to exit.

CHORUS: Hurry!
COYOTE: Come! Before the exits close up forever!

Maude has lost her voice. She mouths and signs her words.

MAUDE: (signs) My voice!
COYOTE: You don't need it!

Coyote reenters, scrambling, grabs Maude, and pulls her out of the still dying, roiling, belching Monster.

One last breath like a death rattle. Then silence.

The Chorus and Coyote stand in sunlight, surrounding Maude.

For a MOMENT, Maude sees Marty, Carrie, and Howard. Overcome with joy, she reaches for them, but they disappear.

Her family goes about their business.

She looks around in growing horror.

Coyote stares up into the sun.

COYOTE: That wasn't easy.
CHORUS 1: Nu
CHORUS 2: Mee
CHORUS 1&2: Poo
COYOTE: We the People. This is how we came to be. The People Crossing Over the Divide.
CHORUS: That's what People do.
CHORUS 1: Nu
CHORUS 2: Me
CHORUS 3: Poo.
CHORUS 1: Let
CHORUS 2: It
CHORUS: Go.

Coyote touches her heart with his pierced paw. They share blood.

COYOTE: Let it go. And live.

The Chorus backs away and out.

Maude is alone.

She attempts to exit.

Stopped by a thicket of thorns. She realizes she cannot leave.

MAUDE: (signs) Let it go.
She is forever altered.

On her knees, she begins to forage.

She disappears into foliage.

Coyote and Chorus reappear and act out the following:

COYOTE: Gather the bones.
CHORUS: And Coyote smeared blood on his hands and sprinkled blood on the bones. Suddenly there came to life again all those who had died inside the Monster. Everyone carved up the great Monster and Coyote began to mete out parts of the body towards the sunrise, towards the sunset, towards the North,

and towards the South. He used up the entire body this way. Then Fox asked –

FOX: What have you done, Coyote? You've given it all away and left nothing for yourself, nothing for us.

CHORUS: And Coyote realized they were right.

COYOTE: (snorts) Well why didn't you tell me this before? I was so busy I didn't think about it. (thinks) Bring me water.

They bring him water. He washes his hands.

CHORUS: And with the bloody water he threw drops upon us all and the land and said

COYOTE: You may be little people because I didn't give you enough of the Monster's body, but you will be powerful and intelligent and brave. You will find your way and learn to live with what you have, and not cry for what you've had to leave behind.

CHORUS: And he named us

COYOTE: Nu-me-poo

CHORUS: The People

They dance and sing.

Maude is revealed encased in thicket.

She resembles the famous Joseph Cornell image of a doll behind thorny branches.

ACT THREE

SCENE ONE

A gravesite.

Next to it, a bush covered with thousands of trinkets, ornaments, mementos, pull-tops, paper clips, rubber bands, political buttons.

Carrie kneels between grave and bush.

Marty enters, unsure and uncomfortable.

MARTY: Is that a grave?
CARRIE: Chief Joseph. (checks pamphlet) The elder.
MARTY: Okay. (points at the BUSH) What's that?

CARRIE: An out-pouring. It's a medicine tree.
MARTY: It's a Christmas Tree on crack. (slight pause) Are you crying?
CARRIE: Of course not.
MARTY: Where's Dad?
CARRIE: I thought he was with you. (slight pause) Should we worry?
MARTY: They already expelled him from the mountain. Where else is he gonna go? There's nothing here but a Post Office, a tourist bureau and a Starbucks.
CARRIE: And the mountain that's got Mom.
MARTY: You make it sound like a monster.
CARRIE: What do you think it is?
MARTY: Her grave marker?

Carrie turns away from him.

MARTY: I don't mean to hurt your feelings. But it's time to come to terms. Pretty soon
I'm going to have to get back to my life. You too.
CARRIE: Not yet.
MARTY: Mom wouldn't like it.
CARRIE: What?
MARTY: Us! We're stuck. Dad is wracked with guilt. You're neglecting your family. I'm about to lose my job.
CARRIE: Don't talk to me about jobs!
MARTY: Life Goes On.
CARRIE: Does it? (holds the pamphlet) This whole place was Nez Perce. This was their holy mountain, but the Wallowa band kinda got screwed out of their birthright. Life didn't necessarily go on for them.
MARTY: Sure it did. There's Indians all over.
CARRIE: Joseph the Younger said, -- (reads pamphlet) "My heart is sick and sad. From where the sun now stands, I will fight no more forever." What kind of life is that? Maybe this is the beginning of the end. Radio says here is going to be a Reckoning.
MARTY: What? Like **2012**!!
CARRIE: Joke all you want. The signs are there.
MARTY: Armageddon starts in Eastern Oregon. Who knew?
CARRIE: Maybe Mom got stuck in some political craziness, some crossfire over ownership.
MART: Wallowa drive-by?

CARRIE: Stop stressing me out!
MARTY: Okay.

Marty removes a doobie.

CARRIE: Not here! How can you, with Mom –
MARTY: She used to do it herself. (before CARRIE
can remonstrate) She did. You know she did.
CARRIE: Those were cigarettes.
MARTY: Hand-rolled. Mom had secrets.
CARRIE: How do you know?
MARTY: 'Cause I do too.

Offers. Carrie wavers.

CARRIE: I don't believe in self-medication.
MARTY: No one's looking. Burn one down for Mom.

Margo lights her up. As they smoke, --

The BUSH, for a moment, seems to come alive.

SCENE TWO
CARDS

The Rescuers play cards.

TUCK: She's long gone.
ASH: What do you mean, gone?
TUCK: Poof!

MEL: Prob'ly down at the Indian Casino knocking
back a couple G&Ts –
TUCK: That's what I'm saying!
MEL: Scarfing down $4.95 Prime Rib –
TUCK: Feeding the one-armed bandit --
FRED: Go Fish.

Tuck fishes.

TUCK: Why doesn't someone go looking for her
there, is all I'm saying.
ASH: (feels her temples as if she has a headache) Stop.
HONEY: He doesn't mean it. Maude's not down at
the casino, we know that.
MEL: (slight pause) She got abducted by aliens!
FRED: Shush!
MEL: With big heads and spidery fingers!
TUCK: MARS ATTACKS!
MEL: She's probably in some other dimension
somewhere getting probed.
FRED: Guys! Please. She's 76 years old!
HONEY: Maybe she can see us but we can't see her,
and she's calling out to us, jumping up and down, but
it's another dimension unknown to our senses,
beyond our consciousness, and even though she's
right in front of us we just walk right through her –
MEL: Go Fish.

Honey fishes.

FRED: (to the others) Drug flashback.

HONEY: Something is keeping us from seeing what's there! And it's the same thing that could make us see, if we would only let ourselves! It's just like riding with the Motorcycle Ministries.

TUCK: Can't we just play cards?

HONEY: "And the Lord said, Go out into the highways and hedges and compel them to come in, that my house may be filled." Luke 14:23. But before I could compel anyone else, I had to compel myself. It must have been like that for you, Tuck, that time you saved those people, --

Tuck sets down his cards. Starts to rise.

ASH: Don't stop!

TUCK: I suck as this game anyway.

FRED: Relax.

TUCK: I don't want to talk about the past, it screws me up. It's got nothing to do with anything.

HONEY: I'm sorry, Tuck.

ASH: Where are you going?

TUCK: Somewhere else. Saving somebody? It's a heavy load, man. I wouldn't wish it on a friend, lemme tell you.

FRED: Tuck, --

Ash rises.

ASH: I'm getting a feeling –

TUCK: Aw geez here it comes.

ASH: I'm seeing her up there, somewhere. But it's like she's a little girl again, in a little knit cap and a matching scarf, real old-fashioned, and it's foggy and cold and she's calling out "Mommy, Mommy" -- but her Mommy isn't there.
HONEY: Ohmigod. That' s tripping me out.

Ash sits, holding her head.

FRED: We got to go up there.
TUCK: Guys, it's over.
FRED: Yeah, but, what if we missed something?
TUCK: We did miss something. *Her.*
FRED: Then let's find her.
TUCK: You of all people. You know it's time to let go.
FRED: Of course I know better. But that doesn't help the way I feel.
MEL: (to ASH, who looks away) Remember that blow-hole thingie in the talus? We shoulda gone in.
HONEY: I'd like to see that.
TUCK: I'm not doing this. Do you hear me? I'm not!
HONEY: That's okay. It doesn't make you a bad person. (to the OTHERS) Can you get free tomorrow?
FRED: Let me check my schedule.

Ash grabs her temples harder than before.

ASH: I need you guys to leave.
HONEY: Getting a migraine? I used to get those too. Especially when I was still using, --

Ash signs for her to be quiet, motioning to her head.

FRED: Let's call it a night.
HONEY: Tomorrow?
TUCK: Guys! I'm not –

Ash motions to her head. Everyone quiets.

They exit.

Ash, no longer hurting, picks up his last hand and plays a card.

ASH: Go Fish.

SCENE THREE

Mary and Carrie finish the doobie.

CARRIE: Aren't you starving?
MARTY: You got the munchies.
CARRIE: I do not!
MARTY: Don't fight the feeling, Sis. Go with it. For once in your life, breathe.
CARRIE: I breathe!
MARTY: Show me.

They breathe together.

MARTY: Good. We're alive. Don't forget that. We're gonna get through this, you and me. It's what life's all about. Getting through.

CARRIE: How is Dad gonna get through?
MARTY: Dad has his own secrets.

Carrie starts laughing.

MARTY: What?
CARRIE: Did you ever wonder about Mom's tattoo?
Where did it come from?
MARTY: Came from before.
CARRIE: Before what?
MARTY: Before Dad.
CARRIE: Before Dad? (giggles) B.D.
MARTY: B.D.!
CARRIE: Her secret life! Biker tats and doobies, --
MARTY: Plus those times she'd go to the car stereo
and crank The Rolling Stones!
CARRIE: The Stones?
MARTY: (sings) PLEASED TO MEET YA/HOPE YOU
GUESSED MY NAME!
CARRIE: I don't remember that.
MARTY: You were too young.
CARRIE: I was with Dad. (looks out) I feel like I don't
know her! I never asked questions. And now I'll
never know the answers.
MARTY: Maybe she didn't want you to know.
CARRIE: Maybe she's full of old grievances and
vendettas that we know nothing about.
Maybe she's like these Nez Perce. Like this grave in
the middle of nowhere that you need a pamphlet to
understand.

MARTY: You don't need a pamphlet to understand Mom. She loves home. And she loves Wallowa. (off her react) You called it a holy place. (RE: the BUSH) Weird. All the stuff we throw away, pop tops and chachkis and ancient history. All this crap. All these memories.

Margo gives the Bush the rest of her rolling papers or even the remaining bud, fastens it to a branch.

CARRIE: All these secrets.

Carrie removes an earring. Puts it on the bush.

MARTY: Really?
CARRIE: It's okay. Mom gave them to me. (giggles) B.D? A.M.
MARTY: What's A.M?
CARRIE: After Mom.
MARTY: After Mom. (puts his arm around her) Let's go get Dad.

SCENE FOUR
3 PART DISCOVERY

PART A
FOREST DAY 13

Tuck listening to SOUNDS, spellbound.

Sound of motorcycle arriving.

Enter Honey and Fred, helmets in hand.

HONEY: Whoa.
FRED: Hey, Tuck. Saw your truck parked at the trailhead.
HONEY: What's going on?
FRED: Pretty counter-intuitive, meeting here in the middle of the week, impossible terrain, that's got to be a class 3 or 4 –
HONEY: And all three of us bumping into each other, I mean – (shivers) It's downright spooky!

Mel enters.

MEL: Whoa.
FRED: What brings you here?
HONEY: I guess you could ask us the same thing.
MEL: Weird
FRED: Unless we're being programmed somehow.
HONEY: Brainwashed?
FRED/HONEY: Ash!!??
HONEY: Ash really is psychic.
FRED: Or just the Mistress of Manipulation.
HONEY: Or maybe we're just all tuned in. I mean, no one told us to be here. We're just here. Even if Ash put it into our heads, they're still our heads!
FRED : Can't sleep, knowing her body is out here somewhere in the rain.
HONEY: Her husband and kids trying to move on. But how can you move on when you don't know what happened?

FRED: So we came one last time.

HONEY: (to TUCK) And we can really use your help!

FRED: Let's just do it, fan out, keep each other in sight and cover as much ground as we can.

HONEY: Come on.

Honey and Fred start out. Tuck doesn't move.

FRED: Tuck?

TUCK: I'm not moving.

FRED: Huh?

TUCK: If I can't find Maude, let her find me.

FRED: You can't find a body by standing still.

TUCK: Nothing else has worked. So let's do nothing.

He takes a deep breath.

Mel and Honey find themselves breathing with him.

Finding their shared breathing, they come to an agreement.

Even Fred starts to relent.

Each sits in his/her own time.

After a moment, Fred stands, fed up. Exits.

After a short time, he re-enters, sits with them.

FRED: Half an hour. Then I'm going.

HONEY: You can't hurry this kind of thing –
TUCK: SHHHH!!!!

Soon they are breathing in unison.

PART B

The three of them sit listening.

Tuck rises, steps away. The other two look his way, shrug.

FRED: Guess he had to pee. (quietly to HONEY) We add oil.
HONEY: Huh?
FRED: Starbucks secret. We add oil to the beans. We buy beans from all over the world, but they have to have the same Starbucks taste, whether you're in Seattle or Tokyo. So we add oil.
HONEY: Crack oil. (slight pause) Thanks.
FRED: For what?
HONEY: Coming clean to me.
TUCK: Guys!

Tuck shows them bones in a tree trunk.

FRED: Yuck.
HONEY: Cool.
FRED: What are they?
MEL: Humanoid. Roughly 150 years old, that would make it 1860s. A complete skeleton or almost.

Adolescent size. Most likely Nez Perce. Skull detached after death.

HONEY: But why's it in the middle of a pine?

TUCK: During water shortage, drought, a pine's roots will reach out for nutrients wherever it can find them.

MEL: A decaying body is ripe for a harvesting.

TUCK: The root grew in, around and through like a snake sucking it's victim dry. Then a big wind or lightning felled the tree, popped the root system and revealed the bones.

HONEY: But why here? The Nez Perce villages were on the Valley side, weren't they? East, facing the Seven Sisters, right?

TUCK: A teenager alone?

MEL: The Wyakin.

HONEY: The who?

MEL: The spirit guide.

TUCK: Acquired as a kind of rite of passage.

HONEY: What? Like a sort of Nez Perce Mitzvah?

FRED: Yeah, I guess.

TUCK: They would go as teenagers alone into the wilderness, no food, no water, nothing but nature.

FRED: After a few days, you start seeing things that aren't there.

HONEY: Or that are.

TUCK: Everything, all things, have a spirit.

MEL: That spirit has a power to share.

HONEY: "Observe all things whatsoever I have commanded you: and lo, I am with you always, even unto the end of the world. Amen." (slight pause) Matthew 28.

TUCK: I would love to buried this way. Surrounded by a womb of roots, my death broken down and taken up into a living trunk and living leaves.

Almost despite himself, Fred reaches out to touch the wood.

Crow CAWS.

PART C

They listen.

In BLACKOUT, Birds and insects transmitting: chirping, tweeting, clicking, ticking. Wind tickling trees, the leisure commerce of daytime wilderness.

FADE UP to shards of light crisscrossing empty space; dust motes flicker; lizards of light dot and dash across the forest floor.

Abrupt utter silence.

Tuck moves deliberate as a drunkard, suspicious. Stops at the edge of a precipice, listens, looks back and uses his hands for signs/gestures:

TUCK: (signs) CAN YOU BELIEVE THIS, NOT A SOUND!

Mel, Honey and Fred migrate, as if on thin ice, to him.

TUCK: (zip lips for silence) HALT.

Flutter of Bird's Wings nearby.

They wait.

CAW-CAW, echoed in a chorus.

Realization from Honey and Fred. Honey points and starts to move in one direction.

TUCK: (signs) HALT, LET'S START DOWN TOGETHER, ON MY SIGNAL, QUIET AS POSSIBLE, FAN OUT AS WE GO. WHEN WE REACH THE BOTTOM, SEARCH TOWARD THE CENTER AND MEET.

FRED/HONEY/MEL: (signs) OKAY.
TUCK: (signs) GO.

They descend.

Then they ascend, into Maude's former hiding place.

Separated, they reorient themselves.

Fred freezes.

Mel, Tuck too caught in freeze frame.

Honey hears a voice.

HONEY: Maude? Maude? Maude.

*Honey slashes through underbrush until Maude is
uncovered. She cradles Maude's head.*

HONEY: Maude? MAUDE!! Look at me,
look...at...me. Water, you need water, here I have
some...

She cannot open her canteen.

HONEY: My God! Open!

*She nearly loses it, has to breathe to grab hold of herself. It
opens.*

HONEY: Your mouth is full of dirt! Let me clear that
crap outa there. Your teeth? Where are you uppers?

*As Maude drunks, Honey rubs her hands up and down
Maude's body, checking for fractures. Maude cries out.*

HONEY: Something here, Maude? Hip? And you're
cold.

Maude hugs her.

HONEY: Oh Maude, you smell like you've been
buried alive.

The word "alive" hits her. She starts to cry.

HONEY: Alive! (calls out) Fred! FRED! She's here! Mel! She's alive! TUCK!!!

Fred, Mel and Tuck join Honey.

FRED: What happened, Maude?
MAUDE: I shouldnta drunk that dirty water.

Fred laughs out loud.

Tuck curls away with walkie-talkie.

TUCK: Twenty one oh seven Franklin, ten eight.

Radio crackles back.

TUCK: Maude found. Alive. Repeat. Maude alive. Bennett Creek area, do you read?

Radio crackles.

TUCK: She is in late stages of hypothermia. Will need ambulance, sled, rope – second thought, alert rappel team, can airlift from Two Colors Meadow....

Looks up at Crows.

TUCK: And tell Sheriff to bring badges, he'll want to deputize some crows.

SCENE FIVE
RETRIEVAL

HOSPITAL ROOM. Maude, wearing a windbreaker, sits in an upstage chair with a suitcase at her feet. Carrie enters in rain gear, shaking out the wet.

CARRIE: Oh my, it'll be raining frogs pretty soon, Mama. We'll have to get going to stay ahead of this squall or we'll be driving blind down the gorge. Dad's signing the release, Marty's parking the car. You ready? Let's put some make-up on, huh? (digs through her purse) Not that you need any.

Carrie finds lipstick. Offers it, but Maude recoils.

CARRIE: Okay. You look great. Different, but great. (shrugs it off) Let's make sure you're all packed.

Reaches for Maude's bag; Maude snatches it up territorially.

CARRIE: Mama! Everything's gonna be okay. Mama?

Howard enters. Marty enters a few steps behind.

CARRIE: Um. Hi Dad.

HOWARD: Did she say anything? (CARRIE shakes her head no)

Maude ignores them.

MARTY: She's got her new teeth in.
HOWARD: Pretty cool, huh? This guy in Baker City read about her in the paper, turns out he's a first-class denture molder.
MARTY: Expensive.
HOWARD: It was on the house.
MARTY: How's her hip?
HOWARD: Healed perfectly. She's ready to roll. (to CARRIE) You're sure she didn't say anything? (CARRIE shakes her head no) I don't think she knows us.
MARTY: Of course she does.
HOWARD: I thought I would never see her again till the Rapture. But God had another plan for us!

He tries to hug Maude. She shakes him off.

MARTY: Mom!
HOWARD: The Maude they found isn't the Maude I lost.
CARRIE: Don't say that!
HOWARD: Sorry, but it's in my heart.
CARRIE: What about what's in her heart?

Silence.

CARRIE: It's *trumoilic* in there.

MARTY: It's what?

CARRIE: So, I invented a word. Turmoil and traumatic.

MARTY: *Trumoilic*. Right.

HOWARD: What are we supposed to do?

CARRIE: Let's just get her home. (tries to soften tone) We'll work through it -- all of us -- together.

MARTY: We're gonna have to.

HOWARD: I just don't know where she went.

MARGO: You mean, in the forest?

HOWARD: In her head. In her heart. (to MAUDE) Where did you go? How did you live? Where did you sleep?

MAUDE: (unused to speaking) In a cow.

HOWARD: What?

MARGO: A cow?

Carrie embraces Maude, who acquiesces.

CARRIE: We got you. Grab hold.

All three help Maude to her feet.

SCENE SIX
REPEAT RETRIEVAL

Replicates Scene 3, reverse point-of-view, Maude faces front, crow stand behind. No dialogue. A stylized, silent version, except Howard, Carrie and Marty seem animalistic, monstrous. Perhaps single words or phrases

241

erupt from silence as if someone were rapidly changing
radio frequencies on a dial.

SCENE SEVEN
PORTLAND

CARRIE watching TV, MAUDE in chair knitting.
Out of the blue:

MAUDE: What did we have to eat last night?

Carrie stunned, joyous.

CARRIE: Baked ham with plum sauce. Scallop
potatoes, green beans, peach tart. Coffee. You had tea.
MAUDE: Who cooked?
CARRIE: Dad did.
MAUDE: It was our anniversary.
CARRIE: Yes. No. That was a long time ago.

Marty enters.

MAUDE: What did we have to eat last night?
CARRIE: Baked ham with plum sauce. Scallop
potatoes, green beans, peach tart. Coffee. You had tea.
MAUDE: Who cooked?
CARRIE: Dad did.
MAUDE: It was our anniversary.
CARRIE: Yes. No. That was a long time ago.

Howard enters.

MAUDE: What did we have to eat last night?
CARRIE: Baked ham with plum sauce. Scallop
potatoes, green beans, peach tart. Coffee. You had tea.
MAUDE: Who cooked?
HOWARD: I did.
MAUDE: It was our anniversary.
MARTY: Yes.
CARRIE: No.
HOWARD: That was a long time ago.

Maude looks at Marty. Maude looks at Carrie. Maude looks at Howard.

The Chorus joins her.

SCENE EIGHT
TWO COLORS

HAPPY BIRTHDAY banner overhead.

A party underway -- Carrie and Margo putter about with food and decorations; Search and Rescuers drink sodas; the Sheriff presides.

Everyone is a little awkward, though glad to see one another.

Honey and Fred embrace.

HONEY: (immediately tearing up) I had her in my arms, had her snot on my sleeve!

FRED: (laughs) You're gonna make me cry!

MEL: Closest thing to Lazarus I've ever seen.

HONEY: Howard told me that Maude used to be a biker chick! She had a hog and everything! I like to think that it kept her alive. That feeling – wind in your face – free –

Maude appears, dressed in knit cap and matching scarf, child-like. Everyone nods at her, keeping their distance out of respect and perhaps a little fear.

DISPATCHER: I believe she slept through the worst of it.

TUCK: They don't sleep.

DISPATCHER: Why not?

MEL: Sleep is surrender.

CARRIE: "If you surrender you will be sorry, and in your sorrow you will feel rather to be dead."

DISPATCHER: Who said that?

CARRIE: Looking Glass to Chief Joseph, just before he surrendered at Bear's Paw, Montana.

TUCK: He'd didn't sleep either.

Howard appears. Removes a speech on a piece of paper.

HOWARD: I just want to thank everyone for coming. Hard to believe it's been over a year since I lost Maude up here, and one full year since you all found her for me. People overuse the word, but my daughters and I can say from the bottom of our hearts that it was a miracle.

He applauds them. They applaud back.

HOWARD: People ask me how's she doing? Well, it's one day at a time -- literally. She doesn't remember stuff that you and I take for granted -- Holidays, polite conversation, what's inside a pumpkin – so everything is essentially new. She used to read books a lot. Now she has to read them again.

Howard sets the speech aside.

HOWARD: She also doesn't seem to remember much at all about who she was. And that means she doesn't really remember us. And that's kinda hard.But there's no pain. She has a good appetite; she's put on a few pounds! She's doing great. We've found a way to come together as a family, and we're just blessed. That's it in a nutshell – we're blessed.

Margo and Carrie emerge with a small cake with a single candle.

HOWARD: So we thought it might be a good idea to come back to the scene of the crime (a look from the SHERIFF) as it were, and celebrate the miracle that connects us all. It's kind of a birthday if you think about it. So let's wish Maude and ourselves a happy first anniversary.

Applause and the beginnings of the Happy Birthday song at war with "For She's a Jolly Good Fellow" until –

HOWARD: Where's Maude?

All look around.

HOWARD: Maude?

EVERYONE: (at their own time and pace) Maude?

Light shift. Maude looks up to see Howard repeating info from the previous speech in distorted manner a la Repeat Retrieval, stressing the words "Pumpkin," "Pain," "Crime," and "Blessed." No one seems to notice but her.

Maude alone in the forest.

She wears warm clothing that somehow makes her look like a little girl.

Distant shouts of "Maude!" that she pays no attention to.

She walks alone till she comes up against briar, barring her path.

She stops. Reaches out. Touches thorns. Makes connections.

FREEZE, as in the Joseph Cornell piece.

END OF PLAY

NoPassport
Press

NoPassport is an unincorporated theatre alliance devoted to cross-cultural, Pan-American performance, theory, action, advocacy, and publication.

Dreaming the Americas Series

Antigone Project: A Play in Five Parts
by Tanya Barfield, Karen Hartman, Chiori Miyagawa, Lynn Nottage and Caridad Svich, with Preface by Lisa Schlesinger, Introduction by Marianne McDonald. **ISBN 978-0-578-03150-7**

Kia Corthron: A Cool Dip in the Barren Saharan Crick and other Plays
(A Cool Dip...Light Raise the Roof, Tap the Leopard)
Preface by Michael John Garces, Interview by Kara Lee Corthron. **ISBN: 978-0-578-09749-7**

Amparo Garcia-Crow: The South Texas Plays
(Cocks Have Claws and Wings to Fly, Under a Western Sky, The Faraway Nearby, Esmeralda Blue) with Preface by Octavio Solis.**ISBN: 978-0-578-01913-0**

Migdalia Cruz: El Grito del Bronx & other plays
(Salt, Yellow Eyes, El Grito del Bronx, Da Bronx rocks: a song) Introduction by Alberto Sandoval-Sanchez, afterword by Priscilla Page. **ISBN: 978-0-578-04992-2**

Envisioning the Americas: Latina/o Theatre & Performance

A NoPassport Press Sampler with works by Migdalia Cruz, John Jesurun, Oliver Mayer, Alejandro Morales and Anne Garcia-Romero

Preface by Jose Rivera. Introduction by Caridad Svich
ISBN: 978-0-578-08274-5

Catherine Filloux: Dog and Wolf & Killing the Boss

Introduction by Cynthia E. Cohen. **ISBN: 978-0-578-07898-4**

David Greenspan: Four Plays and a Monologue

(Jack, 2 Samuel Etc, Old Comedy, Only Beauty, A Playwright's Monologue) Preface by Helen Shaw, Introduction by Taylor Mac, **ISBN: 978-0-578-08448-0**

Karen Hartman: Girl Under Grain

Introduction by Jean Randich. **ISBN: 978-0-578-04981-6**

Kara Hartzler: No Roosters in the Desert

Based on field work by Anna Ochoa O'Leary **ISBN: 978-0-578-07047-6**

John Jesurun: Deep Sleep, White Water, Black Maria – A Media Trilogy

Preface by Fiona Templeton. **ISBN: 978-0-578-02602-2**

Carson Kreitzer: SELF DEFENSE and other Plays
*Self Defense, The Love Song of J Robert Oppenheimer,
1:23, Slither)* Preface by Mark Wing-Davey,
Introduction by Mead K. Hunter.
ISBN: 978-0-578-08058-1.

Lorca: Six Major Plays: *(Blood Wedding, Dona Rosita,
The House of Bernarda Alba, The Public, The Shoemaker's
Prodigious Wife, Yerma)*
In new translations by Caridad Svich, Preface by
James Leverett, Introduction by Amy Rogoway.
ISBN: 978-0-578-00221-7

Matthew Maguire: Three Plays: *(The Tower, Luscious
Music, The Desert)* with Preface by Naomi Wallace.
ISBN: 978-0-578-00856-1

Oliver Mayer: Collected Plays: *(Conjunto, Joe Louis
Blues, Ragged Time)* Preface by Luis Alfaro,
Introduction by Jon D. Rossini
ISBN: 978-0-6151-8370-1

**Chiori Miyagawa: America Dreaming and other
Plays**
Preface by Emily Morse, Afterward by Martin Harries
ISBN: 978-0-578-10189-7

Chiori Miyagawa: Woman Killer
introduction by Sharon Friedman, afterword by
Martin Harries **ISBN: 978-0-578-05008-9**

Alejandro Morales: Collected Plays: *(expat/inferno, marea, Sebastian)* **ISBN: 978-0-6151-8621-4**

Popular Forms for a Radical Theatre
Edited by Caridad Svich and Sarah Ruhl
ISBN: 978-0-578-09809-8

Lisa Ramirez: EXIT CUCKOO (Nanny in motherland) **ISBN: 975-0-578-07520-4.**

Anne Garcia-Romero: Collected Plays:
(Earthquake Chica, Santa Concepcion, Mary Peabody in Cuba) Preface by Juliette Carrillo. **ISBN: 978-0-6151-8888-1**

Octavio Solis: The River Plays *(El Otro, Dreamlandia, Bethlehem)* Introduction by Douglas Langworthy. **ISBN: 978-0-578-04881-9**

Saviana Stanescu: The New York Plays
(Waxing West, Lenin's Shoe, Aliens with Extraordinary Skills) Introduction by John Clinton Eisner. **ISBN: 978-0-578-04942-7**

12 Ophelias (a play with broken songs) by Caridad Svich ISBN: 978-0-6152-4918-6 *(theatre & performance text series single edition)*

The Tropic of X by Caridad Svich
Introduction by Marvin Carlson, Afterword by Tamara Underiner. **ISBN: 978-0-578-03871-1**